I0573953

WYLDBLOOD
MAGAZINE

Issue 1
Feb-Mar 2021

Contents

Wylblood Magazine
Issue 1 – Feb-Mar 2021

Publisher:
Wyldblood Press,
Thicket View, Bakers Lane,
Maidenhead
SL6 6PX UK

Editor: Mark Bilsborough
Fiction editor Sandra Baker
Editorial assistant: Alex Heaton
First reader: Vaughan Stanger

Subscriptions: 6 issues
epub/mobi/pdf delivered to your
inbox £15.
6 issue print subscriptions
available at a discounted rate of
£35 (UK) and £55 (US and
overseas – shipping included)
www.wyldblood.com/magazine.

Single issues available worldwide
via Amazon and from Wyldblood,

www.wyldblood.com
contact@wyldblood.com
facebook.com/WyldbloodPress
t: @WyldbloodPress

Submissions: we are regularly
open for submissions for flash
fiction, short stories and novels –
check our website for our current
status and requirements. We are a
paying market.

Issue 2 available to pre-order now
– published March 2021
www.wyldblood.com/magazine

Editorial

Welcome to the first issue of *Wyldblood magazine* – conceived in one lockdown and published in another, as COVID restrictions become a way of life and there seems to be no end to the uncertainty, disruption and suffering that have dominated the news and our lives.

These are times of enormous change, of course. Whatever happens in the future will be different, and it's hard to escape the feeling that in many ways we are at a turning point, As we stagger into 2021 it's hard to look beyond the pandemic, but the political landscape has been redrawn, the economic hangover of COVID is about to hit and the implications of the looming climate disaster are becoming ever more apparent.

So what a fertile time to be launching a magazine dedicated to speculative fiction in all its forms. We're going to be taking a peek into what's around the corner, and getting our telescopes out to check out what's a long way off. And, because we sometimes need to step back from reality to get a fresh perspective on what's actually true and important, sometimes only fantasy will do.

There'll be all of that and more in these pages. We've got dystopias, utopias, alien races and compromised magic, devil's bargains and fierce loyalties, optimistic futures and harsh warnings. In short everything the future, the past, the multiverse and the imagination can offer.

If that's to your liking, consider taking out a subscription by logging on to our website (www.wyldblood.com) where you can also find new, few flash fiction every Friday in our *Wyld Flash* series. We also publish books so check out our growing range of classics and originals in our bookstore – and watch out for *Call of the Wyld,* our werewolf anthology published next month (and available for pre-order now).

Wyldblood Magazine will publish every two months in 2021 so look out for the second issue in late March, where we've got stories about surviving Mars, never ending traffic jams on the road past ancient Stonehenge and adverts in your head 24/7, plus the usual reviews, commentary and author interviews.

Enjoy,

Mark

Mark Bilsborough
Editor

Coal Dust and Shadows

Holley Cornetto

A dense, uneasy fog had settled over the mountain the day they found the girl in the mine. It crept through hidden cracks and crevices of every home, bringing with it the unmistakable smell of earth and smoke.

Every miner who'd been there told the story differently. Some said she was behind a breakthrough, others that she'd been in an abandoned, half-caved section of the mine. Others still claimed she materialized out of thin air. The one thing they all agreed on is that she was lucky they found her when they did, because that entire section collapsed less than an hour after they extracted her.

My father said when they found her, she was just standing there, as if waiting for them. Her white cotton dress didn't have so much as a smudge on it, and she didn't speak a word.

When I saw her for the time in church on Sunday, I couldn't take my eyes off her. At seventeen years old, I'd never been in love before, but one look at her coal-black hair and pearly-white teeth was all it took. She looked like she'd stepped straight out of a fairy tale.

My little brother, Bobby, leaned close. "I heard she can't talk," he whispered, "and that she's retarded or something."

I punched his leg hard. "Shhh," I hissed. "Don't talk like that."

He wriggled back into the pew and sneered. Bobby didn't like being told what to do. He was two years younger, and we didn't get along well, but Momma always insisted I let him tag along with me.

When church dismissed, I begged Momma to introduce me to the girl from the mine. She gave me a look that was equal parts skeptical and amused. "Well, if she'll be staying in town, it might be nice for her to meet some other young people." She waved at Shane and Bobby. "Y'all come on, too."

Momma led us to the bench where the preacher's wife sat. Reverend Hancock and his wife didn't have children of their own, so they'd volunteered to take the girl in until other arrangements were made. As to what those arrangements might be, no one said.

"Shirley," Momma said, "I was wondering if you would introduce us to the young lady."

I looked down at my shoes, suddenly aware of my greasy hair and the dirt under my fingernails.

Mrs. Hancock smiled and placed a well-manicured hand on the girl's back. "This is Grace. Grace, this is Mrs. Hull, and her son Preston."

"Grace," I repeated, stepping forward.

Mrs. Hancock smiled. "Well, that's what we call her. A reminder to us all that she was saved from that mine by the grace of God."

Grace dipped her head politely in my direction.

I could see Bobby and Shane out of the corner of my eye. I tilted my head in their direction. "This is my brother, Bobby, and my best friend, Shane."

Before Bobby could cut in and embarrass me, Momma put a restraining hand on his shoulder. She shook her head at Mrs. Hancock. "It's a crying shame what happened. Has she said anything yet?"

"Naw, Grace here doesn't say anything at all."

Bobby poked me in the ribs, and turned his most earnest looking expression on Mrs. Hancock. "Can she understand what we say?"

I dug my heel into his foot. He grimaced, but didn't cry out.

Mrs. Hancock chuckled. "Yes, of course she can understand you. Ain't that right, Grace?"

Grace's eyes were as black as her hair. Eyes so deep I thought I might fall into them and keep falling forever. Words formed inside my mind: *I understand just fine.*

I searched her face for some evidence she'd spoken, but her mouth hadn't moved. I glanced over my shoulder at Bobby and Shane, but they looked bored. There was no indication she'd said anything at all, but her expression made clear she'd understood. I must've interpreted that look in my mind and imagined her speaking. My face burned hot.

Mrs. Hancock was still talking to Momma. "Doc Mason says it might be shock, and she may eventually speak again."

It's not shock.

The faint outline of a smile danced across her face as she looked in my direction. I didn't imagine the words. I might have been confused or afraid if I'd thought to question them, but all I could think was that she liked me, too. I cleared my throat and summoned courage I didn't know I had. "Would you mind if I come visit Grace after school tomorrow, Mrs. Hancock?"

"Well, I think that would be just fine, Preston. What do you think, Grace?"

Just fine. She nodded at Mrs. Hancock.

As we left church, Bobby danced in circles, taunting me. I hadn't expected any less from him. I thought Shane might understand, but he seemed preoccupied, muttering to himself with his head down. I caught the phrase "bad feeling" before the rest of his words were carried off by the wind.

I hesitated on the front porch of the Hancock's house, rehearsing what I would say. Before I could knock, the door swung open and Grace emerged in her white cotton dress. I got the feeling she'd been waiting for me. I inhaled sharply, forgetting how to use words.

She smiled and walked down the steps, and I stumbled after her. "I don't know how to ask, but..." I rubbed the back of my neck. "Yesterday, at church... I thought you were talking to me. Like I could hear you in my head

or something." I cringed. That didn't come out the way I'd intended.

She answered with a smile.

"Can you read my mind?"

Of course not.

"There! That! Did you do that? You answered me, didn't you?"

She dipped her head in a nod.

"Do you do that with other people? Can you?"

Just you.

I knew I looked like an idiot, but I couldn't stop the ear-to-ear grin from spreading across my face. "I can show you around town. If you want to, I mean."

She smiled again, and my heart sped up in my chest.

Every day after school, I found her sitting on the porch waiting for me. Some days we walked together in silence; on others I asked her questions. Sometimes, she even answered.

By the following week, we'd fallen into a routine. When I arrived, she stood and looked at me with those coal black eyes. My hands trembled. That much hadn't changed.

Show me the mines.

"Are you sure?" I'd been avoiding taking her there. Baylor had been a mining town for as long as anyone could remember, but I preferred fresh air and sunshine. The thought of being underground nauseated me. It was too confining. When I turned eighteen, everyone expected me to get a job in the mines as my father had done, and his father before him. But I didn't care that mining was the family trade. I wanted no part of it.

She placed her hands on her hips and tilted her head.

"All right, all right." I lifted my hands in surrender and took a step back. "I know a place with a view of the whole mountain. It's a bit of a hike, though, so let me grab some supplies before we go."

We arrived at Hawk's Nest about an hour and a half later. When we reached the clearing, I removed the faded quilt I'd taken from my bedroom, spreading it on the ground for her to sit.

"What do you think? You can see pretty much everything from here."

She was looking toward the mine's entrance in the distance, her brow furrowed.

"Grace?"

They are going to expand it. Drill deeper.

"Yeah." I settled in beside her on the blanket. "That's what I heard, too."

Her jaw was clenched, and I couldn't tell if the shine in her eyes was anger or sadness.

They shouldn't be digging so deep. They're disturbing things they don't understand.

Her words caught me off guard. "Do you mean there's something down there? Did you see something when you were inside?" I thought about taking her hand, about how it would feel in mine.

The mountain was here long before this town, or the people in it. Just because it can't walk or talk doesn't mean it has no spirit, or that it can't feel.

Despite the heat of the West Virginia sun, her words made my blood run cold. "I feel that way too, when I'm out in the forest and there's a stand of old trees. I think sometimes about how long those trees have been there. Longer than I've been alive, or my parents. Longer than my grandparents, even."

She shook her head, but didn't say more.

I put my hand down on the blanket beside hers, just close enough that our fingertips brushed together. "Can I tell you a secret?"

She tilted her head toward me.

"I hate those damned mines. I'd do anything to not have to work in them when I'm older."

Do you have to?

"It's tradition. All the boys in Baylor work the mines when they turn eighteen." I inched my fingers toward her. She didn't move hers away.

You don't want to, though.

I shook my head, and slid my hand over hers. "I'd rather be a farmer. I want to work out in the open air and sunshine."

Her arm jerked, and I cursed myself for a fool. I started to apologize, but stopped when I saw her body convulsing.

I caught her before she collapsed onto the ground. Her eyes rolled back and her body tremored, as if she were having a seizure. I turned her head sideways, and cursed myself for bringing her out here. The climb was probably too much for her.

A loud boom like the crack of thunder sounded below, cascading over the hills and up the mountain. I saw men spill from mine like ants from a hill, shouting and running, chased by pillars of smoke. There was another boom, and a black cloud of dust obscured my view.

By the time the smoke and dust cleared, Grace lay still in my lap.

#

I worried that I wouldn't be able to carry her back down the path, but when I lifted her, she was as light as a shadow.

It was full dark by the time I carried Grace up the stairs to the Hancocks' house. Mrs. Hancock pulled Grace out of my arms and yelled for her husband. They brought her inside, leaving me on the front porch. I sat on the old wooden steps and settled in to wait.

I don't know how long I'd been sitting when the door swung open and Reverend Hancock emerged. He startled when he saw me. "Preston?"

I stood and dusted off my pants leg. "Yes, sir?"

"What are you doing out here? I thought you'd gone home."

I looked past him into the open doorway, but there was no sign of her. "I wanted to make sure Grace was alright."

"There's nothing you can do for her right now. Why don't you go on home, and come back in a day or two, after she's had time to rest?"

I nodded reluctantly and started down the path toward home.

Shane and Bobby caught up with me after school the next day.

"You going to visit your girlfriend again?" Shane asked. "I ain't seen you all week."

Bobby slapped at my books, trying to knock them from my hands. I lifted them overhead where he couldn't reach them. "Naw, she's sick."

"Sick of you, maybe!" Bobby said, jumping to try and tip the books from my hand.

"What's wrong with her?" Shane frowned at Bobby, then stepped forward and shoved him lightly. "Knock it off, twerp."

"Jerk."

"Butt-face."

"She wanted to see the mines," I interrupted, "so I took her up to Hawk's Nest. While we were there, she had a seizure or something."

Bobby thrust his hips. "Was it like this? 'Cause that's an orgasm, dipshit!"

Shane smirked and slapped Bobby on the back of the head. "I don't know why we put up with you." He turned back to me. "Did you hear about the explosion?"

I nodded. "I saw it, actually. I didn't know what it was, though. It happened at the same time Grace started freaking out, so I didn't get a good look. I just heard the boom and saw clouds of smoke and ash."

Shane lifted a brow. "Well, if you ain't gonna see her today, you and me and Bobby ought to go to Clear Creek."

"I'll meet you there." I said, and turned onto the dirt road that led home.

We met at our usual spot, where large, weathered stones lay scattered in the creek bed. We'd spent many hot summer days here swimming and daring each other to jump across the rocks.

Shane lifted a small round stone, bouncing it to test its weight in his palm. "We thought you'd got sick of us." For Shane, conversation was like haggling. He started with an unlikely proposition, then worked his way toward the heart of the matter.

Bobby jumped in and sent a spray of water in my direction. "Your girlfriend's a freak! She only likes you because she's soft in the head."

I clenched my fists and started after him, but Shane grabbed my shoulder. "Let it go. You know how he is, he's just talking shit."

Shane offered me the stone in his hand. I took it and flipped my wrist in one fluid motion, sending it skimming across the water's surface.

"So, you really like her, huh?" He tossed another stone in after mine. He looked out across the water, counting the times it bounced off the surface.

It was an unspoken rule not to look each other in the eyes when we talked about something serious or embarrassing. Given the heat on my cheeks, I was grateful for the rule. "I do."

"How d'you know you like her if she never says anything? I mean, she's pretty and all, but don't you get bored with all the silence?"

I glanced across the water and spotted Bobby upstream, using my shoe to catch minnows. I pretended not to notice. The last thing I needed was for him to overhear. "There's something I wanna tell you, and I don't know if you're going to believe me. It sounds crazy."

Shane sent another stone skipping across the surface. "You know I'll believe you. You don't lie. Hell, you don't even exaggerate."

"She *does* talk to me."

Despite our rule, Shane turned to me in surprise. "You mean she's been able to talk all this time and--"

"No. Not like that. I mean, she says things *in my head*." Unable to meet his eyes, I studied the stone in my hand.

"Preston…" From the corner of my eye, I could see him glance upstream. Satisfied that Bobby was out of listening range, he continued, "What does 'in my head' mean exactly?"

I ran my thumb along the rock's smooth surface. "I can hear her… in my head. But her lips don't move, and no one else can hear it."

Shane ran a hand through his hair. "Are you trying to tell me she's telepathic?"

"I… I don't know." I sat down on the boulder, dangling my feet in the water. "I asked her, and she said she can't read my mind, or anything weird like that."

Shane chuckled. "Right, because *that* would be weird."

I suddenly realized how ridiculous it sounded, and I laughed with him. "You aren't going to call me insane?"

He rubbed his chin. "I told you I'd believe you, and I do. But I don't know what, exactly, I'm believing here. There's definitely something strange about her. You remember the seizure you told me about?"

"Yeah."

"Well, that ain't the first one she's had. My daddy said she had some kinda fit after they pulled her out of the mine. Shaking and foaming at the mouth. Right around the time the shaft they found her in collapsed."

I dropped a stone into the water. What he was implying didn't make sense. "What are you trying to say?"

"I don't know. Just… something is weird about all this. Before she showed up do you know how long it had been since there were any big accidents at the mine? Twenty years. Twenty! But after she shows up, suddenly there are two major accidents in a week. It ain't normal, Preston."

Shane prided himself on knowing everything there was to know about the town's history. He couldn't wait for the day he was old enough to plunge into the depths of the mountain and baptize himself in its darkness. If he said twenty years, I believed him.

"Hey!" Bobby yelled. "Are y'all gonna come swimming or not?"

I shook my head. "I think I should head home. Give me back my shoe, asshole."

He waded further into the creek, holding my shoe over his head.

I grumbled under my breath and headed in after him.

I couldn't concentrate the next day at school. I kept one eye on the clock, and tried to calm the butterflies in my stomach. Around one thirty, Vice Principal Childers came in and called several students out of class. Usually stern from breaking up too many fights over the years, Childers showed no trace of anger, only concern. The entire class seemed to hold their breath as he listed off the names. Shane was called second to last.

I knew only one thing could have affected that many students. When the bell rang for dismissal, I jumped from my desk and ran straight to Shane's house.

His little sister was on the front porch when I arrived. I doubled over, trying to catch my breath.

"Are you looking for Shane?"

"Yeah, he got called out of school. Is everything okay? Is he here?" My t-shirt clung to pools of sweat on my back. I used the collar to dry my forehead.

"He's inside. I'll get him. You don't want to go in there." She vanished behind the screen door.

Her words sent a shiver down my spine. A thousand scenarios ran through my mind. Maybe I was wrong and there wasn't another accident. Maybe someone was sick. Contagious.

The door creaked, interrupting my speculation. Shane stepped onto the porch. He looked tired, drained. "Preston." Something in his tone made me feel like an intruder.

"You left school today. I was worried."

"There was another accident at the mine." His eyes flickered upward. "Daddy and some of his crew got trapped inside."

It felt like the wind had been knocked out of me. "Are they... alive?"

"They don't know yet. They're drilling, trying to break through and make contact." Unshed tears glinted from the corners of his eyes.

"Shit, Shane, I'm so sorry."

"Have you seen Grace today?" The muscles of his jaw tightened when he said her name.

"No, I came straight here. Why?"

"Because, I want to know if she had another one of her damned fits! I want to know if she did this!"

"Shane, that's..."

"Impossible? You're the one that told me she spoke to you in your head." He jabbed his finger into my collarbone. "She's some kind of witch, or demon, or God-knows-what, and I want to know if she made this happen."

"How could she? She's just a girl, Shane. And a sick one, at that." He wasn't thinking clearly. He was upset about the accident. He needed someone to blame, and he'd picked Grace.

"You go see her, Preston. See if she's still sick. Then come back here and tell me she didn't do this."

If I couldn't reason with him, I could at least see Grace to prove his theory wrong. "Okay, I'll go."

For a moment, I thought I'd only imagined her sitting on the steps. The angle of the sun blanketed her in shadow, leaving her little more than a silhouette. "Grace?"

When I spoke her name, it was as if those shadows took tangible form, and she was again herself. But that was silly, just my imagination playing tricks. A large basket sat beside her, and as I glanced at it, she pushed it aside.

Not yet. It's a surprise.

For a moment, she almost made me forget my promise to Shane. "So, then... you're well today? You didn't have another seizure or anything?"

My fever broke this afternoon. I woke up and felt fine.

"What time did you wake up?"

She looked up at me, and I saw myself reflected in her eyes. She scooted away just slightly, and crossed her arms over her chest.

"I'm sorry. I should've said I'm glad you're okay." I offered her my hand.

She lifted the basket and took my hand. This time she led me, taking me down to the path toward the creek. She took the long way; one I didn't often travel. I noticed the soles of her feet flashed black when she walked, as if covered in coal dust.

We stopped at a thicket of mountain laurels, where she spread a blanket and unpacked the picnic she'd prepared. I watched her unpack fried chicken, coleslaw, and lemonade. All my favorite things, though I'd never told her. I wondered for a moment if she'd lied about reading my mind.

"Grace, there's something I need to ask you."

She nodded and took my hands in hers, pulling me down to join her on the blanket. The sunlight glimmered off the white dress she always wore.

I settled in beside her and shook away my distraction. I had to make good on my promise to Shane. "Do you know anything about the accidents at the mine?"

Her lip quivered. *I thought you hated the mines.*

It was neither confirmation nor denial. I'd have to approach the subject another way. I took a bite of the chicken. "Thanks for this," I said after swallowing. "You got all my favorites."

By the time we finished our picnic, the sky was growing dark. She scooted closer and took my hand.

There were so many things I needed to ask her - about the mountain and the mines, about her seizures and her fever, about how she knew my favorite things to eat. But before I could organize my thoughts into words, she took my cheek in her hand and leaned forward.

As we kissed, my questions dissolved. All words were lost to me, useless to express the things I felt. A thick fog seeped from the earth to shroud us in its curtain, shutting out the world.

Some might've called what we did a sin, and if it was a sin, it was one born of love. Afterward, I lay on the blanket beside her, my nose pressed against her hair, breathing in her scent of earth and smoke. My heart felt as though it would burst. I couldn't remember a time when I'd ever been so happy.

I wrapped my arms around her as if she were some phantom girl who might, at any moment, become a part of the fog that surrounded us. In that moment, I knew I had lied to Shane. She wasn't *just* a girl. She was something else entirely. "Grace," I whispered, "tell me about the mines."

They come with their drills and bring destruction.

"I know, but those men are innocent."

I thought you hated the mine too, I thought you'd understand.

There was a bitterness in her tone that caught me off guard. It was cold and hard, like the mountain.

"They do what they must to provide for their families." There was more I wanted to say, but the heavy fog surrounding us made my head feel light.

She settled in against me, and we lay together in quiet stillness until I fell into the blackest depths of a dreamless sleep.

I couldn't tell how long I slept, but when I woke, the blanket beside me was empty. I sat bolt upright and looked around the laurel thicket, but saw no sign of Grace. I grabbed my clothes and pulled them on with shaking hands. I trembled not with cold, I realized, but with fear.

"Grace?" I took a few steps toward the edge of the laurels.

Silence.

Maybe she was afraid of being caught out late and snuck home. The more I thought about it, the more it made sense to me. She'd tried to wake me but couldn't. Or, maybe she wanted me to rest.

When I got back to our picnic site, I noticed that her side of the blanket was covered with a fine layer of black dust.

I woke the next morning in my own bed, my head pounding out the rhythm of my heartbeat. My sheets were caked with grime and dried blood. Cuts covered my legs from groping my way home in the darkness. I didn't remember walking home. I must have, but I couldn't remember.

The telephone's high-pitched ring made my head feel as if it were splitting. I stumbled into the kitchen and lifted the receiver. It was Shane.

"They got them out, Preston. They're all going to be okay."

The miners. Memories of yesterday's events flooded back. "I talked to Grace about the accidents. I don't think you need to worry anymore."

"Grace?" He asked.

He must've forgotten in all the excitement. "Yeah. Remember yesterday? You said you thought that she... might have something to do with the accident."

"Who's Grace?"

My heart sank. It wasn't like him to play pranks, especially considering what he'd been through these past few days.

"Look Preston, I'm sorry, but I need to go. I have more calls to make. Talk to you, later."

"Yeah, later," I tried to answer, but he'd already hung up. I stared at the phone in my hand as if it could give me answers.

"Who was that on the phone?"

I jumped at the sound of my mother's voice. "Shane. He said they rescued the men who were trapped."

She filled a mug with coffee and sat down at the table, patting the place beside her. "I heard. Your father went to visit the hospital this morning. But that's where the good news ends, I'm afraid."

"What do you mean?"

"An inspector came in to investigate the recent accidents. They've decided the best course of action is to close the mines."

My head pounded with the echo of Grace's words, but in a voice I did not recall. It was an ancient sound, a deep rumble like shifting gravel. *I thought you'd understand.*

"Grace."

Momma tilted her head. "What, honey?"

"Grace. She hated those mines."

She shook her head. "Who is Grace?"

"The girl they pulled out of the mine. The girl staying with the Hancocks. We met her at church, remember?"

"They didn't pull any girl out of the mine. Not that I know of, anyway. When did you say this happened?"

"Just last week, Mom."

She pressed the back of her hand against my forehead. "Do you feel alright?"

"I'm fine."

"You're burning up. I think you must've had a fever dream." She led me back to my bedroom and tsked when she saw the dirty sheets. "I'll never understand how you boys are always so filthy!" I sat on the trunk at the foot of my bed while she grabbed fresh linens.

Why would Mom and Shane act like they didn't know Grace? Why pretend she never existed?

Mom turned down the bed and held up the blanket. "Get settled in. I'll bring you something to bring the fever down."

I nodded. I hoped I was dreaming, that I'd wake up and find myself still in the laurel thicket with Grace. I closed my eyes, and fell into a fitful sleep.

Each time I woke, someone different stood over me: Doc Mason, my parents, Shane, Bobby. I tried to ask about Grace, but no one answered. No one remembered.

The doctor was sitting at the edge of the bed when I came around. "You had us all worried for a while there, young man." His tone was matter-of-fact. "You've had a severe fever, and hallucinations."

"Hallucinations?" I asked.

"You kept asking for someone named Grace."

I swallowed. The inside of my mouth was like a desert.

"You may be weak for a day or two longer, so take it easy until you feel like yourself again." He patted my knee, and left me to my thoughts.

Eventually, I recovered. No one spoke of the hallucinations again. When I tried to bring it up with my mom, she simply said I was sick, and it couldn't be helped.

No one remembered Grace. After a while, I began to wonder whether or not she had been real. Even now, when I try to conjure her image in my mind's eye, her form darkens and shifts as if she weren't of flesh and bone. As if she were made of coal dust and shadows.

Holley Cornetto has stories in or forthcoming in over a dozen magazines and anthologies, including: *Daily Science Fiction* (2020), *It Calls From the Forest* (2020), *Scare Me* (2020), and *The Half That You See: Nightmares, Deliriums, and Illusions* .(2021), among others.

Thawing

JL George

The ice princess watched over us from her plinth in the city square, crystalline, inviolate, and perfect.

The first time I saw her, I was a child, tugging restlessly at my father's hand as we waited for Mother to finish up her business in the city. The day had dragged on longer than expected, forcing him to spend money on hot tea and handcakes from the vendors who lined the square. My ears were cold and I was tired of walking, grizzling and complaining endlessly—until the clouds parted and allowed through a pale beam of winter sun that glittered on her face.

I stopped, transfixed, and Father hoisted me into his arms, glad of the distraction. "Did I tell you the story of Princess Eira?" he said. "No? Well, it's about time I did."

A long time ago, the tale began, the city of Dinas Uchaf and the lands around it had been ruled by kings and queens. Over time, their power diminished, and the elders of the city made most of the decisions, but their descendants continued to live in the palace. They gave the inhabitants something to be proud of, Father explained. They were a living reminder of our heritage, our traditions.

Princess Eira had been wise, and kind, and discontented with sitting in the palace wearing fine silk dresses and putting in appearances at state events and galas. She took to walking among the people in ordinary clothes, talking with them in the streets, and they, all unknowing who she was, spilled their troubles to her as they did to their neighbours. And then she took to petitioning the Council of Elders, begging for help for the poor and the hungry, giving her own wealth to feed and clothe them and send their children to school. The people adored her.

But there was another problem. The ice dragons of the north moved ever closer to the city, encroaching on the outlying villages with their frozen breath that killed the crops, decimating the farmers' herds with their talons like knives of ice. Dinas Uchaf had always been cold, with snow on the ground even in summer, but the dragons threatened to make it an uninhabitable wasteland. All the fighting men and women of Dinas Uchaf couldn't hold them back. They would retreat only if offered a sacrifice.

Eira knew what she had to do. She rode forth beyond the city walls—for in those days it had been a fortress, much smaller than today's sprawl and bounded in on all sides—into what was now the square. There she came face to face with the greatest and fiercest of the dragons. The ground froze where his feet touched it and his breath, glittering with ice crystals, deadened the trees. Eira lowered her eyes, accepting her fate, and with a single exhalation he froze her solid where she stood.

She has stood here ever since, watching over Dinas Uchaf and its people. They say that should the ice ever melt, the city will fall and the ice dragons come howling back to claim it.

Father winked at me, then. "That's what they say, anyway. It's only a statue. Still, better not touch it, hm? The custodian'll tell us off."

I nodded, but my eyes lingered on the ice princess's face, its expression of stoic acceptance, the unseeing crystals of her eyes. To have stood there untouched, for so many years. She must have been so terribly lonely.

Each time my parents took me to the city, after that, I begged to be allowed to see the ice princess. And each time, they smiled and let me stand at the foot of the statue, my hands hot inside my gloves, knowing the statue would melt were I to touch it, and itching to do so anyway.

They assumed the fascination would fade as I grew older, but it never did. I wore out my friends with staring at her when they were more interested in visiting the stalls around the square or flirting with the sons and daughters of the market traders. My ambition was one thing only: to become custodian of the square, so that one day I should be the one to take care of her, to sweep the snow from the steps around her statue and tell her story to staring children.

Mother and Father thought it a child's fancy, at first, but it did not pass, and when I reached an age to leave home, they sent me to the city to be apprenticed.

Old Anna, the custodian, was brisk at first, barking at me for daydreaming when I paused too long to gaze upon the ice princess. But as the months wore on her demeanour softened. "You're a hardworking lass, I'll give you that," she allowed, at first. And a few months later: "You care for her, don't you? The princess?"

I held myself still, fearing she'd seen something unseemly in my attachment to the statue. It was a thing I held close to my chest, fearing that the light of scrutiny might melt it like a snowflake on the tongue. "That's our job," I said.

Anna lifted an eyebrow. The effect, on her weather-beaten face, was that of someone having drawn a sceptical expression on a brown paper bag. "Don't come that with me," she said. "And don't talk like it's something to be ashamed of. Princess needs her guardian, and that can't be me much longer. My bones ache in the cold." She flexed an arthritic hand for emphasis, knuckles cracking.

My heart leapt. That night I sat up late in the square, the snow settling on my hair and my shoulders, and talked to the ice princess. "I think old Anna means to retire soon," I told her. "Will you miss her, I wonder?" I frowned and tipped my head back. The clouds had parted to reveal the Pole Star, bright and lonely and terribly far away. "She'll miss you. I know that."

The ice princess stayed where she was, that same immovable expression on her face. The longer I spent around her, the harder I found it to read. When I was young, listening to Father's stories, I'd thought it the quiet acceptance of somebody resigned to her fate. Now I imagined the hint of a smile in it sometimes; other days, an incipient frown.

I imagined her eyes followed me across the square as I returned to the custodian's hut, tracing the trail of my footprints in the snow; but when I turned back, at the last, her gaze was fixed blankly upon her folded hands.

Old Anna retired at the midwinter solstice, saying it was a new year, and time for a new custodian. My parents came to the city to celebrate my promotion. We ate lunch in a real restaurant, and I drank a cup of wine that stained my lips and made my head feel light and expansive.

As I returned to my bed, I saw a figure in the square, near the ice princess. I opened my mouth to shout, but then I recognized the stooped form: Anna, taking her leave.

I stepped back into the shadows of the square, aware I was intruding on something private. Anna lingered by the statue—talking to her, perhaps, though too quietly for me to hear. She reached up, then, and placed her hand lightly on the clasped ones of the princess.

My breath caught in my throat. Never touch her with bare hands. Your warm skin will melt the ice. I'd known that since I was small. It had been the first lesson Anna had drilled into me, too, and I'd been scrupulous in observing it. Yet here she was, her ungloved hand curling around the statue's as though she was taking her leave of an old friend.

I waited, holding my breath, for Anna to leave. She would stay with her nephew and his wife tonight, now the custodian's hut was no longer hers. It might take her a while to find a place in the city that her pension would cover. She'd talked about going south, back to the farming village where she and her sisters had

been born, where the air was clean and the streets quiet. I hoped she would be happy, wherever she went.

Back in the custodian's hut—my hut, now—I curled up beneath my blankets and slept fitfully. Perhaps it was the wine, or perhaps the hut was too quiet for comfort without Anna's stertorous breathing. My dreams were sharp and strange.

The ice princess at night, but this time it was I and not Anna who reached out to take her hand. The ice princess toppling from her pedestal and smashing to smithereens on the flagstones. The ice princess, but not made of ice at all. She was a living woman with pink cheeks and yellow hair, and she reached for my hand and murmured, "Call me Eira."

I leaned in toward her, but before our lips touched, the dream broke and I woke shivering. I had forgotten to close the window last night, and there were snowflakes clinging to my eyelashes.

Late the next day, the last few stallholders closing up shop in the square, I brushed the snowflakes from the ice princess's shoulders. I'd never thought of it before, but using the brush felt impersonal, distant. Before last night, how long had it been since somebody had touched her?

I chided myself for the thought. She was only a statue, after all. The real Eira had given her life for the city many years ago.

But before I left to secure the barriers that would protect her for the night, I laid my gloved hand softly on her shoulder.

She did not turn to water on the spot, as some irrational part of me had feared. She stayed as she had always been: cold, unmoving, lonely.

I dreamed of her again that night. In the dream, she stood in sunshine, wearing a dress that bared her freckled shoulders, and her skin was warm beneath my hand. At my touch, she turned to face me, her eyes full of sorrow.

"I've been trapped here so long," she said. "It's so cold."

"What can I do?" I heard myself say.

She placed her palm against mine, interlacing our fingers. "You know what to do," she told me.

"I can't," I said. "You'll melt, you'll vanish."

Eira put her head on one side. "Who told you that?"

It took me a while to pluck up the courage. Weeks of brief, hesitant touches with gloved hands after dark; weeks of the same dream, where Eira urged me to set her free and I protested.

I told myself it was my imagination. Without old Anna around to ground me, my mind was playing tricks on itself. The ice princess in the square was only a memorial. Perhaps if I visited the real Eira's grave, it would set my mind to rest.

The next time my father came to the city, we sat at the foot of the statue drinking hot tea, and I broached the subject with him. "You remember when I was small? And we were right here, and you told me the story of Princess Eira?"

Father smiled, the wrinkles at the corners of his eyes creasing up. "Of course. I could never get you to concentrate for two minutes at a time, but that story? You listened to the whole thing without so much as looking away."

"But you didn't tell me everything."

He frowned. "What do you mean?"

"The ice princess—the real princess, I mean. Princess Eira. What happened to her? I mean, where did they bury her?"

"You know, I don't think I know. One of the old crypts under the city, I suppose."

Mother didn't know, either. Neither did old Anna, when she next came into the city to visit her nephew. Neither had the elders of the city council who paid my wages, or any of the visitors who stopped before the statue to tell their own children Eira's story.

The next time I had the dream, I took a deep breath and asked her, "What did you mean? When you asked who told me about the statue?"

She took both my hands in hers. "I meant what I said. Where did it come from, that story? Who does it serve?"

"It came from my father. And he heard it from his parents, and I suppose they heard it from theirs." I shrugged. "It's an old tale. Everybody knows it."

"Everybody knows," she echoed, "yet none of them were there." She looked into my eyes. "And my other question? Who does it serve?"

I shook my head. "I don't understand. It's just a story about how the city came to be."

"Every origin story serves somebody," Eira said. "Think about who's telling it. Who isn't here to speak."

"You."

"Me. I'm frozen in time. Voiceless. And the story ensures I stay that way. The ice melts, the dragons return. And we wouldn't want that, would we?" Her voice hardened, an unfamiliar, sardonic twist to her mouth.

"But nobody really believes that," I pointed out. "It's a statue, in the square. Even children know. Father told me so when I was little."

"And yet the city pays you to ensure that the ice never melts. That the dragons never return."

"They're not real," I said. "It's just a story."

"It's just *half* a story."

The humans had won; the ice dragons had left. The story said that it was peaceful, and right. Of course, nobody had seen a dragon near human habitation in a hundred years. We couldn't have asked them if we'd wanted to.

I almost didn't dare ask; but I had to. "What really happened?"

"Walk with me."

Eira took my hand, and in the dream, we wound our way between young trees with lemons ripening on their branches, the lush grass soft beneath our feet. I'd never seen such things in the waking world. This had to be somewhere down south, nowhere near Dinas Uchaf.

"The dragons were here before us," Eira said, at length. "Their migrations last for years, and in their absence, humans found this place and built a city on it. But it had been their home for thousands of years. Hundreds of thousands."

I blinked. "I didn't know that."

"Nor did I, until I was old enough that Father gave me free rein in his library. I went straight for the histories that were censored elsewhere, of course." She gave a short, bitter laugh. "The dragons had begun to be an issue—that was how they put it—when I was very small. I'd grown up hearing adults bicker over how we should deal with the problem. Imagine my surprise when I learned that *we* were the problem, not them!"

I didn't need to imagine it. I supposed my expression gave that away. Eira went on, her eyes distant. "Imagine my even greater surprise when my father—my kind, gentle father—advised me to tell no-one of what I'd learned. It didn't matter, he said. This was our home now. The dragons had chosen to leave it behind; they could hardly return and claim it again."

"But they tried."

"They did. And I couldn't keep silent forever. After Father died, I begged the Council of Elders to talk to them. To bargain. Even to abandon the city and rebuild anew in the south! They refused, and so I took my concerns before the people."

"The people loved you," I said, recalling what Father had told me. "That part was true, at least?"

"Many of them did. Some disagreed. There was great division in the city, and the dragons were upon us, and I did not know what to do. But the council of elders had an idea."

Her expression darkened and she fell silent. I squeezed her hand in encouragement.

"They managed to capture a small dragon. A juvenile; the offspring of the leader. They threatened to kill her if the dragons did not leave the city to stand. And, to ensure they stayed away, they demanded their participation in a binding magic. A spell that would keep them from the city as long as it lasted." Her voice trembled, just briefly. "It did, I'm afraid, require a sacrifice. And there was somebody they very much desired to get out of the way."

Her eyes brimmed with tears, and mine did, too. The city I'd longed to live in, the statue I'd longed to protect—it had been a lie. All of it, a lie.

Eira took my face in her hands. "Your parents don't live in the city."

I shook my head. "They fish. They live on the coast, to the southeast."

"Good. Then you have a place to run to."

"Run…?"

"You know what to do," she said, and pressed her lips to mine; and this time it was true.

This time, I was running across the square before I was even fully conscious I was awake.

The early-morning walkers looked at me strangely, but I spared them not a moment's thought. I made for the statue.

No: for the ice princess.

I wrapped my arms around her and pressed kisses to her lips, and felt the ice begin to melt at my touch.

Above the city, a cold crack of lightning. Fear coiled in my chest as I raised my eyes and saw the blizzard that was coming, the great shapes, diamond-white, that roiled within it.

Somebody took my hand.

I whirled, and there she was, standing beside me. A princess of flesh and blood and warmth and rage, free at last from her cold prison. She surveyed the city around her.

"Eira?" My voice wavered.

"Let it freeze," she said, at last.

The storm was upon us now, and hand in hand, we ran.

JL George is a speculative fiction writer from Cardiff. Her work appears in Fireside, Curiosities, Constellary Tales, and various other places, and her novella The Word will be published by New Welsh Rarebyte in 2021. In her other lives, she's a library-monkey and an academic working on classic weird fiction and the Gothic. You can find her at www.jl-george.com.

The Butcher's Dog

Peri Dwyer Worrell

He sold me, but I'm sure it was a mistake.

I sat erect under the corrugated metal roof over the Mercado 28 de Febrero in Cuenca, Ecuador. All the other market dogs dropped their tails, curled their ears, and slunk around me – and quite rightly. I barely even acknowledged them (unless there was a bitch in heat, of course). Why should I? My sleek fur and soft contours clearly demonstrated my superiority, in contrast to their dull coats and gaunt ribs.

My privilege and dignity were due to my loyal, loving, and natural devotion to Hector, the butcher. The booth I guarded at night was set up each morning, filled with delectable whole chickens, pigs' sides hung on hooks above the swine's heads on the counter, and heaps of scrumptious ground beef. For breakfast, I lapped blood from the concrete before it disappeared down the drain in the floor. I nabbed scraps of skin and fat that flew when the cleaver whacked flesh on the gouged and stained wood block.

The customers came day in and day out: stocky, serious *indigenas* buying chickens complete with feet and head; restaurateurs who'd buy an entire half pig and minutely oversee the cuts; every now and then a rich *gringa* who'd demand all fat be trimmed away, the feet and heads discarded. The last were my favorite.

Hector took their money and gave them their meat. One day, instead of meat, he took a man's money and instead of meat, he gave him me.

Perhaps I should explain my background. First, I'm of a herding breed. Think of a border collie, or an Australian shepherd. Then think of generations of my ancestors weaving our way through the untidy traffic of Andean towns. The dullards among us don't survive to breed. I don't mean to brag, here. It's just a simple

statement of fact that we're among the smartest dogs in the world.

My mother was in charge of herding an entire rural flock, mixed goats and alpacas. It was poetry in motion to watch her agility as she guided them along the steepest ravines, or expertly cut the very one the owner desired out of the flock. One morning well before dawn, when I was not yet a year old, I pranced along at the heels of the herder's son. He was on his way to sell fat goats for slaughter.

The meat wholesaler, Raul, eyed me with admiration. His gaze kept falling on me during his preliminary small talk with the youth. I stared back.

I followed the transactions easily, watching hands and faces, nods and body language, smelling the puffs of social pheromones. When their business was done, it was clear that I'd been part of the transaction. I licked the boy's hand, once only, and crossed to lie down at the meat distributor's feet. But that ownership was brief.

Around sunrise, I trotted out of the warehouse, a few inches behind the left heel of the next customer. He was a retail butcher — Hector. Raul threw me in on a bargain that Hector had pressed him hard on.

No need to be indignant! This happens to pups, at least the worthy ones among us who aren't driven out into the streets or thrown off cliffs in burlap bags. This is a poor country, and pets are a luxury.

I followed Hector to Raul's loading dock, where I sat silently, ears forward. Watching him supervise the carcasses loaded on his truck, I assessed him as forthright, calm, and fair. He struck me as an alpha with nothing to prove. His body odor bespoke moderation but not abstention.

I approved of the man. I was content with my fate. When loading finished, at a nod from Hector, I jumped into the truck's cab and took my place on the passenger-side floorboard.

That first glorious day at the mercado, I could hardly believe my luck! At dusk, we returned to Hector's home, a walled compound of wooden buildings on stilts, set into a hillside. His children ran up squealing to meet the new dog. After ear-scratching and hand-licking, I investigated a hutch of cuys, little edible rodents that they kept for holiday meat. Hector's wife eyed me warily as I sniffed the free-ranging chickens until she was satisfied that I wouldn't kill one. When it got cold that night, I found a warm spot next to the kitchen wall where the fire was banked in the corner and curled up for the night.

I was home.

But when this event of which I speak happened, I was five years old, already in love with Hector, proud of my place in the market at his feet, reveling in the daily carnivorous feast, basking in the sunshine in the thin mountain air. I felt sure I was set for life.

Then the gringo Charlie walked into the *mercado*. I knew him as a regular customer, smelling, as usual, like too much mint and not enough garlic, combined with a chemical disinfectant smell I intensely disliked. Today he also smelled just recovered from a cold, overlaid with the lovely funky sweat of recent sex. Visually, he looked soft and pale, as always, and he laughed his normal, harshly nervous laugh that set my neck hairs twitching. However, I ignored the laugh and wagged my

tail, drooling, because he usually pinched off a tiny piece of ground meat and flicked it to me right after Hector weighed it. He picked out his meats for the week and spoke intently with Hector. I gave a tiny yip of surprise when I realized by their looks at me and their body language, the smells of Hector's reluctance and greed and the gringo's determination and triumph, that I was part of today's deal.

When it was done, Charlie clicked his tongue.

"Mashi," he called me. I followed, stiff-legged, looking repeatedly back at Hector, expecting him to change his mind, but he ignored me. The smell of his regret was the only goodbye I got.

To add insult to injury, when I walked past the seamstress's booth down the aisle, the fragrance of my distress emboldened her creepy little dachshund. He darted out and nipped at my hind leg, an impudence he'd never have tried the day before. I snarled and pinned him with a paw. His yips and growls attracted everyone's attention. The seamstress whipped a scrap of velvet at us, and he scrambled back.

Charlie grabbed my scruff and spoke sternly to me in English. He slipped a collar around my neck and clipped a leash to it, the first time I'd ever been bound. I shook my head and backed up, but finding myself captive, I followed him. This did not bode well for my future.

Charlie took me to his home, a second-floor suite facing the courtyard of a colonial building. I lived indoors, an odd arrangement. We went out every day for a walk in the neighborhood. I didn't understand the English words of his commands at first, but his meaning was usually clear. "Sit" was "*siéntete*," for example.

He'd walk with me each morning to the city park, cautioning me to "Stay... Stay.... Stay," every few seconds, until finally...

"Go!" I would spring forward and race up and down the grassy meadows. Charlie would ignore me. I would pause on a small rise at the end of the park closest to the *mercado*, sniffing the air for all the smells there, but especially for the meat smell. When I caught that iron blood aroma, I examined it for the slightest trace of Hector's familiar odor.

I found out that Charlie's chemical smell was concentrated in a room at the end of his suite. He entered it only after donning booties, plastic gloves, a coverall, and a plastic face shield. When Charlie went in there, I lay across the doorway and waited, sometimes for hours of solitude and boredom. I was trying to be a good dog for Charlie, but I missed Hector.

One day, we came home from our early-morning walk and Charlie disappeared into the room. He came out after a short time holding a syringe.

"Here you go, boy!" he said. I wagged my tail, since that was his phrase when he tossed me a scrap. But instead he knelt, pinched up the skin on my neck, and injected me with the syringe. "You're officially CRISPRed!" He gave his jerky laugh.

I felt odd immediately. My heart beat faster and I felt like I might vomit. I stumbled to my plush bed in the corner and lay down.

I slept the rest of the day; it was twilight when I awakened. My throat was sore and my nose was dry. I shook my head and immediately regretted it as the room spun. I reeled to my water bowl and lapped up so much water that I did vomit a little, which hurt my sore throat terribly.

Charlie stood over me, writing in a notebook. I collapsed on my belly then, and after a few minutes he scooped me up and carried me back to my bed.

I stayed in that bed for a few days, turning up my nose at the meals Charlie put in front of me, often putting my paws over my eyes to block the painful daylight, my ears folded to block the normal city sounds, now acutely amplified. A couple of times, Charlie disturbed me to draw blood from my foreleg, but that barely registered through the fog of pain and nausea.

Eventually I began to feel better. One morning, I still had a dull headache, but I was ravenously hungry. I walked over to my untouched meal from the day before, chicken offal, *mote*, and broth, and began to eat.

What a strange sensation as I worked my tongue and teeth! As a dog, I had no lips to speak of, but my mouth muscles quivered oddly around my jowls and chin. When I swallowed, something in my throat I'd never felt before quivered.

Charlie noticed I was up.

"You're eating, Mashi! Good boy!" I beat my tail on the floor. "Is that good, Mashi? Is it good?"

As spontaneously as my tail wagged, I raised my head and made a noise. It wasn't exactly a bark.

"Goooo," I said.

Charlie's eyebrows shot up. His smell signaled excitement. He grabbed his notebook and scribbled something.

"Mashi." My tail thumped again. "Is that...*gooooooood*?" He drew out the sounds carefully and my eyes were drawn to his mouth.

My mouth and throat seemed out of my control as I formed the syllable back at him, "Gooooo." I was unequipped for the "d" sound so I ended the word with a short, shrill yip.

"Yes!" Charlie made a fist and did a little dance. My tail thumped. Suddenly I was exhausted again. I walked to my bed and collapsed, leaving Charlie to scribble.

As I regained my health, we resumed our daily walks. I gradually built my endurance back up in the park. I never stopped pausing on the rise, and now I tried to form the sounds of his name, "Hector" as I sniffed the breeze.

I regained the weight I'd lost, though my coat was never as lush as it had been when I was the butcher's dog, king of the *mercado*.

Charlie grew irritable. Mainly it seemed, he was angry that he couldn't tell anyone about me.

"Mashi," tail thump, "they wouldn't understand, would they, boy?" He'd scratch my ears. "But you're the proof aren't you? Might even outlive me, won't you? And you're a *real* best friend, aren't you a real best friend?"

"Veshk ren(yip)," I'd answer. *Best friend.* Each time I tried to make a phoneme my mouth was unsuited for, I got a little closer. But a full nasal stop while voicing was still tricky for me. And my changing face refused to grow lips.

Now, dogs don't lie. That's part of why people love dogs, I think. But a really smart dog, such as, for example, a herding breed that's been naturally selected for cunning over generations, can mislead, withhold information, or redirect.

I quickly realized that Charlie thought I understood no more language than I could speak. But the truth was, slowly as my body was changing and allowing me to approach intelligible speech, my brain was outpacing it exponentially.

"We'll just have to repeat the blood test a little earlier this week, won't we?" Charlie would muse. A lonely man, he spoke to me a lot. I let him think it was in the nature of talking to himself, but inside my head I was thinking, *you'll probably do it Tuesday instead of Thursday because you're seeing Elena on Thursday this week, aren't you? And Wednesday is your cards night.*

"We'll do it Tuesday. Yes, we will. Who's my good boy?" Tail thump. "Is it Mashi? Is Mashi a good, good boy?"

"Goo(yip) oy." *Good boy.* I walked up to him for an ear rub, but he was already engrossed in his computer.

I missed Hector.

Then came the day Charlie drew blood from my foreleg, then followed it up with an injection that made me fall asleep.

I woke inside a small box with mesh windows. The latch was a simple mechanism. Charlie knew by now that I was smart and determined enough to undo most latches,

limited only by my lack of thumbs, so he'd added a combination lock.

The box was inside a vehicle, an SUV, and Charlie sat next to the driver. I lay quietly and watched the sky on one side and cliff faces on the other as we wended our way down switchbacks. A few times I spotted alpacas and thought nostalgically of my mother. Finally, after descending many thousands of feet in altitude, the road straightened out onto Ecuador's coastal plateau.

In another hour or two, we stopped at a busy location (which I now know was an airport). At the time, the smell of aviation fuel, thousands of people from all over, the ocean breeze, and the glorious stink of the city of Guayaquil were overwhelming, strange and new. I stood inside the crate, yearning to get out to explore, but instead a stranger loaded the crate on a cart and left me to sit in the unfamiliar equatorial heat for hours.

I was eventually loaded into the belly of a plane. The noise was incredible, reminding me of those first post-CRISPR days when my head felt like it would burst. But soon the air became thin and dry and cold again, like Cuenca, and I settled into an uneasy sleep.

I'll skip the transition through Customs and the trip to Charlie's house. Suffice it to say, I was confused and withdrawn during the whole ordeal and for days afterwards.

Charlie's home was huge by Ecuadorian standards, though I gathered from comments he made on the phone to his friends and family that it was normal for the US. I disliked the laminate floors in the living area intensely, for both their plasticky odor and the way my toenails scraped on them, so I spent as much time as I could on the kitchen tile or in the carpeted bedrooms.

But the wonderful thing about Charlie's American home was that it had a backyard that opened onto a power-line easement that stretched for miles! Several times a day, I'd stand by the back door.

"Run!" I'd say.

"You want to run? You want to run? Sit!" Charlie would reach for the doorknob. I'd obediently sit, quivering with anticipation.

"Stay!" he'd say, while he opened the door.

I'd freeze.

"Go, Mashi! Run!"

I'd dash out the door, pause to work the latch on the back gate, and race for miles up and down under the power lines. Sometimes I'd meet a human jogger, try to herd a giggling group of children playing, or chase a cat briefly. I'd encounter other dogs and we'd butt-sniff, play bow, and run back and forth a few times, but as a herding breed, I wasn't as much of a pack animal as most dogs. But there are no words for the joy I felt in running as fast as I could, as far as I wanted. In those moments, I was free from the strangeness of the creature I'd become, no longer dog, not quite person.

I was also free of the deception of pretending to be stupider than I am.

Finally, Charlie would put two fingers in his mouth and whistle. I might be miles away by then, but I'd hear, turn, and race back.

I think those runs were all that saved me from losing my mind.

Charlie worked as an independent laboratory safety consultant (ironic, considering how many regulations he'd violated by performing his CRISPR on me). His various contracts around the Dallas area where we lived often required him to go to work every day for weeks or months, but the rest of the time, he spoke with other humans by phone, if at all.

In Ecuador, he'd been forced to visit the crowded *mercados* for food, and he'd had a weekly card game with other English-speaking expats. He'd even had an Ecuadorian girlfriend, though her pregnancy (I could smell that the baby was his, but he didn't believe it. I remained tactfully silent on the matter) was what precipitated our sudden move. But here, he ordered groceries and anything he needed online, including a call girl every couple of weeks.

I was the only one he spoke to, many days.

"Good boy, Mashi! Is he a good boy?"

"Goo(yip) oy!" I'd respond.

"Here's a cookie!" He'd give me a treat, one of the fishy, brothy-tasting crisps I loved.

I understood what he was doing. *Two can play at that game*, I thought.

One day while he was at work, I dragged a runner from the carpeted bedroom to the detestable laminate floor. When Charlie came home, after he'd let me out for my run, he moved the rug back where it had come from.

"Who's a good boy?" Charlie asked expectantly.

I stood looking at him, wagging my tail.

"Who's a *good boy*?" he asked, slower and louder.

I clicked my poor toenails across that heinous laminate to the bedroom and stood, looking at him, next to the runner. He followed me.

"Who's a good boy?" He tried again. I slowly wagged my tail but didn't move, holding his gaze, summoning the alpha authority of my days as king of the *mercado*.

Slowly, it dawned on him. He picked up the runner and put it back, forming a bridge across the clicky, smelly laminate so I could cross from carpet to tile without touching it. I marched proudly across the bridge and stood by my food bowl.

"Goo(yip) oy!" I said.

Training Charlie went well after that. Some things he knew I was teaching him to do, like leaving a few treats on the counter so I could help myself when he was at work.

"Treats." I pointed at the counter with my nose. Once he figured out what I wanted, he seemed amused. I rewarded him with a new vocabulary word each time.

"Chair," I'd say, hopping on and off the kitchen chair.

"Ook," nudging an open book on the coffee table.

Other behaviors took longer to reinforce, because he had no idea he was doing them. Leaving his computer logged into voice command mode, for example. I had to wait for him to enable it, which he only did occasionally. Then I chattered my way through all my vocabulary words and tossed in a few new ones. It took three or four months of that, and about forty new words, before he started leaving voice command on all the time. After that, it took a number of redirection strategies before he got in the habit of leaving it on in the morning when he went to work.

Now I was cooking, as they say. Though, no, I never felt any urge to learn to cook. Dogs are almost without exception raw-foods enthusiasts. Cooking smells are just a signal to us that humans are handling food and we'd better get in there and get our share.

I always feel the urge to learn, though. And in an era of instant e-learning online, a talking dog with a voice-activated computer is all set. There was a bit of a learning curve on the computer's part while it learned to deal with my, shall we say, idiosyncratic accent. And there was a panicked near-miss one afternoon when the garage door opened and I almost didn't get the web browser shut down in time.

After that, I started a program of talking more, immediately on his entry, when he took a long time to get out of the car and come inside. That was such a subtle behavior to reinforce it took many months to noticeably slow his transition time. After a year or so, though, he was consistently sitting in the car and sipping a beverage, flipping through social media on his phone, before coming inside.

Much less stressful for me.

By the time I turned eight, I was talking with Charlie using the vocabulary of a bright three-year-old human. I had finished 6th-grade math and introductory computer science, and worked my way, backwards, through world history to the 6th century on Chan Academy. I had several e-mail accounts. Being, as previously mentioned, thumbless, I had to wait

with vigilance and patience for Charlie to leave his credit card lying out, but by that time I had fair control over how much he drank each evening. When he laid the card down by the keyboard and poured himself a scotch, it was a simple matter of tail wags, nudges, licks, a couple of new words, and so forth to lead him to drink seven or eight of them. He staggered to bed and fell in with his clothes on, so I dragged the quilt over him to make sure he'd sleep soundly. Then I went back and memorized the card information, front and back. I carefully replaced the card where he'd left it.

As I surfed online more, I began to look at Charlie's wardrobe critically. Though he had PhD in biochemistry, and seemed to have adequate clientele, I could tell that he was pushing the boundaries of acceptable attire: worn flip-flops, chinos that were faded and frayed. Here in the USA, home of giant portions and sugary drinks and snacks, his polo shirts had begun to stretch across his belly unflatteringly. I burrowed into his closet and drawers, exhuming shirts in larger sizes, loafers, and dress socks, laboriously repacking his wardrobe so they were a little more accessible. Occasionally, I even dragged a particularly threadbare or tight garment out to the trash barrel when he was at work on trash pick-up day, though I risked one of the neighbors noticing and mentioning it to him. I logged onto his user accounts and searched for hours for business-casual clothing so he'd be inundated with ads for dressier trousers. His ad feed was now full of photos of men posing gazing off the pier in yachting clothes, or standing by a big desk in a corner office in crisp professional attire. Then, one night, I made a real sacrifice to achieve my goals: I chewed up his flip-flops.

I won't lie: I enjoyed it. I *am* a dog, and the combined flavors and aromas of leather, rubber, and toe jam were scrumptious. But, unlike stupider dogs, I fully understood that I would be scolded and punished for it. I may be a standoffish herding dog, but I *am* a dog, and being yelled at and having my nose smacked, followed by being locked in my crate, was an emotionally difficult experience for me, even knowing that it was for a good cause.

But my sacrifice was rewarded the next day when he finally donned the loafers that I'd tugged just far enough out of the back-bottom corner of the closet so that he could spot them. Now I had a master whose appearance I could at least be somewhat proud of, even if he was an unethical, awkward boor.

It made me miss Hector even more: Hector, the butcher, the *don* of the mercado, a true *caballero*, respected by the *indigenas* in their velvet skirts, beloved by all the almond-eyed children, so respected he was sometimes asked to mediate petty disputes. Hector, always forthright, always upright, and always kind.

One day I was out on my run when I caught the whiff of a bitch in heat. It had been a long time for me, and this one had a healthy aroma. My nose took over my body, my mind along for the ride, and I veered to the smell's source.

Which was an eight-foot privacy fence segregating a yard from the power-line easement. For a dog of my agility, all it took was a running start. I leapt in the air, fully committed. My feet scrabbled up the top few feet of the fence, my momentum carrying me to the top. My front paws hooked over, my back claws dug in…and I was in the yard with a gorgeous female Rottweiler. It was one of the most joyous matings of my life. The Rottweiler's owner looked out her window just as we finished and came out, yelling, to chase me away. The human grabbed the Rottie's collar, causing her sleek brown and black coat to ripple. I grinned and simpered against the gate, hoping to avoid any unpleasantness. The human let go of the bitch and closed in on me.

"Smart one, aren't you?" she asked.

You have no idea! I thought.

She opened the latch and I was out. I felt relaxed, invigorated, alive! It didn't even dull my mood when I heard Charlie's whistle just at

that moment. I turned my path towards his home.

Things went on this way for several more months. Charlie, with his improved image, got better clients and steadier work. He even began to socialize a bit, leaving me alone longer on weekend evenings.

I progressed in my studies, but still I yearned for Hector. Then I reached the Chan Academy lessons on the Olmec and pre-contact Andean civilizations and my homesickness began to throb palpably.

It was then that I began to formulate a plan.

So, here I am. It turned out to be almost absurdly simple, really. I created an online account with a special service for exporting pets to foreign countries. After a thousand or so attempts, I held a pen in my mouth and forged my vet's signature on the required certificate of health. Today, the appointed pick-up date, I dragged my crate out onto the porch, stacked the paperwork neatly on a wicker loveseat, weighted it down with a rock, and climbed into the crate.

I'm sitting here waiting for the transport truck to pull up. The address for delivery is the butcher of the *mercado* on *Calle 28 de Febrero*, Cuenca, Ecuador. My crate is to be released on the signature of one Hector.

And, to make my triumph complete, I can smell a litter of newborn, half-Rottweiler puppies on the breeze. Apparently, one of the amazing things about CRISPR is that it alters the germ line of future generations. If I'm not mistaken, the Rottweiler's mistress will be quite taken aback one day when she talks to the puppies.

And they talk back.

Peri Dwyer Worrell *has a keen appreciation of diversity, tolerance, and taking no crap from anyone. After 30 years as a physician, Peri expatriated to Latin America, where she writes and edits.*

A Gleam of Gold

Dorothy A Winsor

Wind slid down the chimney and out through the fireplace to ruffle the hair Jarka had beaten into neatness that morning. *Very funny*, he told it silently. *You're hilarious.*

"Whenever you're ready," the dormitory master snapped. The skin sagging from his jaw lifted as he pressed his lips thin.

Jarka wrapped his left hand around the strap of the bag carrying his wind box. Tightening the right one on his crutch to keep it from slipping on the polished floor, he hitched to where the master waited with the leather curtain pulled aside. The master gestured Jarka through into a space that resembled a jail cell more than the room where Prince Beran had stashed him for the last three weeks. But the prince had left for the Westreach that morning, so here Jarka was. When a prince took you in, you slept where you were told. In this case, one of the two beds standing across from one another. Jarka recognized the bag holding his clothes slumped on the floor.

"Yours." The master pointed to the bare mattress on the left. "I'll send someone with bedding." He lifted a forefinger, a pose Jarka had seen before in people about to deliver a lecture.

Lie low, he reminded himself. *You don't know where trouble's lurking here.*

"I'm told you lived on the streets before Prince Beran took pity on you," the master said.

"Prince Beran didn't take me in out of pity," Jarka interrupted. When the dormitory master raised an eyebrow, he hurried on, "He found out I'm a wind reader, and he wants me trained to be his advisor when he becomes king some day." He set the leather bag on the bed and tapped the swirling wind rune on its flap. "That's why he gave me the wind box."

"There'll be none of that barbaroc magic in the dormitory," the master said, voice sharp.

Jarka kept his face as bland as possible. He knew most folks thought like the master did, that magic was barbaric, and civilized folks believed only in the Divine Powers. It had taken him a while to realize they didn't even feel the elemental energy all around them.

The master drew a breath, then continued more calmly. "Also no sneaking around after curfew. And no thieving," he added as an afterthought.

Thieving? Jarka took an instant to swallow the insult. "Fine."

"Yes, master," the master prompted.

"Yes, master," Jarka said through gritted teeth.

The master waited a few heartbeats as if to be sure Jarka was sufficiently ground down. "Your roommate is Dugan. He'll be along presently. He can answer questions." The master shoved out past the curtain, but looked over his shoulder to add, "Make yourself at home."

Jarka suppressed a snort. At home? So far, the castle felt more like another gang's territory. Still, if he stayed out of trouble, he'd be sleeping inside and eating regular meals. That was worth listening to a lecture or two. Also, the castle library held more books than he'd ever seen in one place before, and he meant to read them all.

He lifted the lid of the chest at the foot of his bed and dumped his few clothes in. Then he untied the flap of his carry bag to check on his new wind box, nestled beside the small velvet pouch of colored paper bits. Even collapsed to fit in the bag, the box filled him with the same awe he'd felt when Prince Beran gave it to him. Jarka had known he was a wind reader since he was twelve, but until now, he'd made do with a box woven from reeds. He ran his hand over one rune-covered slat. A tremor of power stirred under his finger. Hastily, he shut the flap.

The curtain rings rattled, and a boy of maybe eight shuffled in, eyes barely visible over an armload of bedding.

"Dugan?" Jarka asked, lifting the load and spilling it on the bed. Should he be insulted to be given a little kid as a roommate?

The boy rolled his eyes. "Sweet Powers, no. I sleep in the pages' dorm. I'm Finar." Now that the kid wasn't buried in blankets, Jarka could see he wore a page's tunic that wasn't laced all the way and had slid off one skinny shoulder. Around his neck, he wore a thin chain dangling a gold rune of protection.

Finar might look a little like a neglected street kid, Jarka thought, but the gold proclaimed he wasn't one. "I'm Jarka."

"I know. Everybody does. You're Wyswoman Adrya's new apprentice." He smiled as if the idea pleased him.

Jarka moved his carry bag carefully to the floor and fished one-handed for a bedsheet.

Finar eyed his crutch. "You want help?" he asked then quickly added, "It's hard for everybody to get the sheet tucked in on the wall side."

Jarka considered claiming he could do it himself, but Finar had already moved most of the bedding to the top of the clothes chest and shaken out the sheet. So Jarka gave in and caught the edge closest to him. He'd had just finished smoothing the top blanket when a tall, broad-shouldered boy pushed past the curtain, stopped, and stood with his feet apart and his hands on his hips, filling the doorway. Dugan,

Jarka guessed and groaned inwardly. He'd seen much less well-fed versions of this boy on the streets. Their arrival was never good news.

"What are you doing here, Finar?" Dugan demanded.

"Helping Jarka." Finar slid the protection charm back and forth on its chain. "You know. The one Adrya actually chose to be her apprentice."

Actually chose? Had Adrya been considering someone else?

Dugan took two steps and stopped within a foot of Finar, looming over him. "That old woman is too stupid to know talent when she sees it."

Oh, stone it. It was him. Jarka had hoped he was through with sleeping with one eye open.

"I'm getting ready to write to my father," Dugan said bending his face close to Finar's. "He'll be interested in how we're getting along." Dugan flicked a look Jarka's way. "Finar's father is my father's vassal. My father sets his taxes."

Finar jammed his hands into his armpits, hugging his narrow chest.

Dugan held the curtain aside. "Out."

Finar scuttled away. The curtain dropped behind him.

Dugan turned to Jarka. "I don't know what you think he was implying, but he's a little liar." Dugan's eye fell on the flap of the carry bag holding Jarka's wind box. He took a step back. "What's that?"

"My wind box." Jarka refrained from rolling his eyes. He knew from experience that lots of people feared magic, feared what unknown thing it might be able to do. His cousin's new husband had been frightened enough to drive Jarka out onto the street. That was when he'd decided to treat his wind reading as if he was a fake offering entertainment. That way, he scratched the itch to read without risking himself too much. Until Prince Beran came along, of course. He'd recognized what he saw and lured Jarka into the open with the offer of books. Given that instinct for which bribe would work, Jarka cynically figured Beran would make a good king someday.

"You're not going to keep that thing here, are you?" Dugan asked.

"Wyswoman Adrya said I had to so I wouldn't spook folks." That was the truth. "Of course, I can have it out when I'm reading whatever secrets the wind has collected that day." And that was a lie, though the wind did collect secrets as it swept over the world. "Want me to read for you?" Jarka lifted his eyebrows brightly. Needling this thug was hard to resist.

Dugan blinked. "You better not."

Jarka didn't really blame him. Secrets were dangerous. That was why they were secret. And that was undoubtedly why Prince Beran wanted Jarka. He tried not to think about it.

He bent to scoop up the bag, set it gently in his chest, and shut the lid. "If you don't want me to, I won't. Don't touch it though. It's not safe." He hitched toward the doorway, deliberately making Dugan back out of his way.

"Make trouble for me with that thing and I'll get you thrown back into the gutter," Dugan cried.

"No trouble from me," Jarka called over his shoulder. Given Beran's absence and the master's warning, it was possible Dugan really could get him tossed out. He'd starved and slept in abandoned buildings quite long enough, thank you very much. Making trouble was the last thing on his mind. He started off for the library and today's lesson with the Wyswoman.

When he headed back to his room, Jarka carried a book. "Read the first half," Wyswoman Adrya had said as if she were assigning a chore.

"Note the hard choices kings and their advisors have to make." He rubbed his thumb on the smooth cover. He had all afternoon to read, and then there'd be supper.

He swung around a corner and nearly ran into Finar, who had one side of his tunic hiked up and was poking at a bruise on his ribs. Finar jumped and hastily dropped the tunic.

"Where'd you get that?" Jarka asked.

"I fell." Finar turned away.

Jarka had seen bruises like that before, some of them with his own shirt lifted. They came from fists. "Was it Dugan?"

"Of course not." Finar tried to duck past him. When Jarka stuck out his crutch to block his way, Finar hopped over it. "Leave it alone. You'll just make trouble." He sped away.

More slowly, Jarka continued to the dorm, where he hitched past the row of curtained doorways to the better light of the window seat at the end of the hall. *Leave it*, he told himself. *Finar says it's nothing. Maybe that's the truth. Or maybe the trouble is done. Anyway it's not my trouble.*

He sat and slid off his shoe to rub his crooked foot, aching from the chilly autumn weather. Until the day she died, his mother had insisted his foot was a sign he had a gift. "The Divine Powers never take anything away without giving something back," she'd claimed. She hadn't lived long enough to see his wind reading blossom. He pressed his foot back into his shoe. If wind reading was a gift, it was one he'd paid for. He settled the book in his lap.

Wind leaked around the edge of the window pane. *You have to wait until tomorrow morning*, he told it. *I'll read you before everyone else is up.* He opened his book, determined to enjoy it, but wind flung grit against the glass. It wanted something from him.

Power, it whispered. *Hard choices.*

He dropped his head back against the wall behind him. Stone it all, anyway. As the book Wyswoman Adrya had given him made clear, power and hard choices were Prince Beran's business. But not Jarka's, not yet.

Jarka's stomach pressed against his belt. Supper had been even better than he hoped. He pivoted on his crutch, slid the curtain to his room aside, and stopped dead. A small figure was bent over Dugan's clothes chest, digging through it.

"What are you doing?"

Finar whirled to face Jarka. The chest's lid banged shut behind him. "Nothing."

For a moment, Jarka was tempted to buy the lie. The thing was, Finar might not be a street kid, but at this moment he was as unprotected a kid as Jarka had seen. He weighed his options. Maybe he could inch his head out above the parapet just this one time.

"Something up with Dugan?" Jarka asked.

Finar's chin trembled. "He took the necklace my mother gave me when I left home, and I need it, and I can't find it."

Sure enough, the necklace with the rune was missing from the kid's neck. In the hall, something blew loose and clattered to the floor. The bellows always propped against the chimney, Jarka guessed. He sighed.

"Then we have to make him give it back."

"Could we beat him up?" Finar sounded hopeful.

Finar had obviously never learned the wisdom of the streets, Jarka thought. "I don't know about you, but he'd pound me to jelly. We have to scare him off."

Finar's eyes widened. "We should use your wind box. He's frightened of it."

Jarka's heart tripped. Finar had no idea what sacrilege he was asking for. This kind of risk was not what he'd agreed to. Not yet. Still, the kid needed him. "Dugan would never let me read for him," Jarka said slowly. "We have to trick him." He'd scramble the ritual, Jarka decided. He'd proved for years on the street that he was good at fakery. The wind probably wouldn't even notice.

Finar bounced on his toes. "Tell me what to do."

The entrance to the dormitory opened and, to Jarka's relief, Dugan came through it. Jarka didn't need boys from the other cells or, Divine Powers help him, the master asking what that foot long square was under the blanket on the window seat.

Dugan sauntered toward him. "Why are you hanging around out here?"

Just a little closer, Jarka prodded silently. Dugan took two more steps, and Jarka whipped the blanket aside, revealing his wind box. Rune covered oak slats gleamed in the fading sunlight, the gaps between them waiting for the wind to push through, arrange the paper bits, and spill what it knew. Not that it would do that now of course, he reassured himself. This was just playacting.

Dugan froze, the color in his face fading to ash.

Jarka hastily grabbed the velvet pouch and dumped multi-colored confetti into his hand. He had to be fast before Dugan had time to notice anything.

"The Powers move in the wind," Jarka intoned. "Wind sweeps between Earth and Sky. It whispers of where it's been and where it's going. I humbly beg you, Mother Earth, Father Sky, use the white of the North Wind." He flung paper bits into the box.

"Why is that thing out?" Dugan squeaked.

"The blue of the East Wind, the red of the South Wind, the green of the West Wind, tell me who took Finar's necklace." Jarka flung paper with abandon. Bold fakery was good fakery. He blew into the box, then pretended to examine the piles of paper. "Dugan?" he cried. "Really?"

Now, Jarka silently urged.

A burst of wind puffed Dugan's shirt away from his body.

"He has to give it back or you'll blow him off the top of the castle?" Jarka went on.

Dugan turned as if to run. Then, to Jarka's dismay, he rocked to a stop, grabbed the closest curtain, and dragged out Finar, holding the bellows from the fireplace. He shook the kid hard enough that Finar's head snapped back and forth. "You! Both of you are going to be sorry. I'm telling the master." He let go of Finar and charged down the hall.

Wind howled from the fireplace, swaying the whole row of heavy curtains, and hitting Dugan hard enough to spin him around.

Jarka nearly fell off the window seat.

Finar staggered a step backward but still was gutsy enough to shout, "Give it back or you'll be the one who's sorry."

From the corner of his eye, Jarka saw movement in his wind box.

Dugan fished in his pocket, pulled out a gleam of gold, and threw it at Finar.

Jarka turned his head to look in the box where paper bits had swirled into hills. Wild wind swept into his head, loaded with elemental energy. The dormitory hallway blurred. He felt ice on his tongue. His nostrils filled with the smell of damp earth. He was dimly aware of Dugan fleeing the dorm, but in the glowing center of darkness, emptiness spread out all around him. Before he could grasp what was happening, wind slapped the side of his head. *Fake? Ha!*, he heard. *Stand up straight!* The darkness fell away, and the dorm took shape around him, smelling of dirty socks and pastries smuggled from the kitchen.

He stared into the wind box. That... should not have happened. And "stand up straight"? Posture advice? He tapped his crutch on the floor. Was that a joke?

"Jarka?" Finar tugged on Jarka's sleeve. Jarka had the sense Finar had said his name more than once. "Thank you," Finar said. He slid his necklace over his head and ran out of the dormitory.

Jarka scooped up the paper, collapsed the wind box, and fumbled it all into the leather bag. He'd faced down hunger, beatings, child fiddlers, and soldiers with drawn swords. None of them had been as terrifying as what just happened in this supposedly safe castle hallway. He'd thought he might be in danger from Dugan. It occurred to him now that maybe Dugan wasn't where the real danger lay. He'd touched power here, just as he'd be expected to touch it, to learn secrets, for Prince Beran.

He couldn't help believing he'd done a good thing for Finar. But was power ever a thing to be cleanly used? What had he got himself into with Beran and this beautiful wind box that called to him even now?

Too late, the wind burbled.

I have to give you that one, he thought.

He hitched to his room and placed the box in his clothes chest as gently as he would have placed a sack of black powder. He took out his book and sat on the bed. He'd read, not the wind but ink on a page making words that shaped the world and made sense of things. Yes, that was what he'd do. The pages shook when he turned them. And yet, inside, he felt an ember of hope spark into life. This was what he'd been born for.

In an empty space in the wall behind him, wind danced like a child who'd been given a present.

Dorothy A. Winsor writes fantasy novels, including Deep as a Tomb (Loose Leave Publishing, 2016), The Wind Reader (Inspired Quill, 2018), The Wysman (Inspired Quill, 2020), and The Trickster (Inspired Quill, 2021). She lives near Chicago.

Bargaining with Frogs
Stephanie Kraner

In a time of glorious kings and handsome princes, a time of witches and silent, painted women, there lived a princess who thought all of it was rubbish. Her father, the aforementioned "glorious" king, had made three attempts to arrange her marriage to a prince – handsome or otherwise – from a distant kingdom, thereby increasing his own wealth and lands. However, each of these three attempts had ended with some embarrassment and a more than a little rage on the behalf of all involved.

The first ended when the pompous, presumptuous prince had cornered and tried to kiss her after the betrothal. They were walking together towards the grand staircase, and he just shoved her up against the wall, all fish-lips in her face. Princess Solveig grabbed the first thing that came to hand – in this case, a brass candlestick – and swung it at the side of his head with all her might. He released her, she fled to the safety of her room, and he and his entourage stormed out of the kingdom the next day. She heard he had quite the lump to show for his unwanted affections.

The second didn't even last to the end of the betrothal feast when he grabbed two of the servant girls, pulled them into his lap, and then pawed at them in front of all the guests. The princess saved the poor girls, who were clearly afraid to defy a prince but also did not seem to want his hands on them. She picked up a flagon of her father's best burgundy and dumped the entire contents over his head. The girls, unfortunately also hit by the spray, were at least able to get away, and the prince cursed her for a madwoman and left immediately.

Then there was the third prince, the haughtiest of all. *That* prince looked her up and down as though she were a breeding mare at auction. Her face flushed with anger at the way his squinty, watery eyes traveled the length of

her body, but before she could voice her disgust, he refused the wedding agreement. According to him, she was not pretty enough to satisfy.

Princess Solveig actually laughed aloud at his pronouncement, and despite her father's evident fury at her behavior, she felt no shame in pointing out the prince's uncanny resemblance to the ostriches in her father's menagerie.

Not wanting to be subjected to any further princes and their monumental egos, she ran away. In her haste to leave, she grabbed only her diamond circlet, her emerald ring, and her necklace of lapis. These, she figured she could sell to pay for a room to sleep in and bread to fill her stomach. Her father would, of course, send hunters after her, so she headed west into the woods.

For a full day and night, Solveig traveled without stopping. The thick brush tore at her skirts and errant branches scratched her face and the skin of her arms. At times, she thought she heard footsteps behind her, but when she crouched amid the ferns, she saw no one in pursuit. The more time that passed, the more confident she felt that she'd escaped, but she also grew concerned that she couldn't find her way out of the woods.

When she came upon a crumbling, abandoned well, she stopped to rest. Though the shade of the woods kept the air cool, sweat beaded on her brow. A moss-covered wooden bucket attached to a rope sat next to her, so she picked it up and tossed it into the well, smiling when she heard it splash. She hauled it back up and used the water to wipe her face and sate her thirst. As she drank from her cupped hands, a small voice called up from the wall.

"What brings a princess this deep into the forest?"

She jumped back, sloshing a considerable amount of water all over her. "Who's down there?" she demanded.

"Just me," said the voice. "I live in these woods. Not many people venture this deep, and none of them are princesses."

Solveig peered over the side, squinting into the inky darkness. "I'm not a princess," she said. "And it's none of your concern what I'm doing here."

"Begging your pardon, my lady," the voice said. "That circlet on your head says otherwise."

"Fine," she said. "I'm not a princess *anymore*." As she spoke, she leaned farther over the side of the well to try and make out who could possibly be speaking to her, but when she did so, the lapis necklace caught on a ragged piece of stone and came unclasped. She tried to grab it as it fell, but it slipped through her wet fingers and splashed into the water below.

"Drat and curses!" the princess shouted. "What are you doing down there anyways? Come out where I can see you."

"As you wish," said the voice.

Another splash echoed from within the well as something emerged from the water, and after a few moments, during which the princess retreated several paces, a fat, slimy frog climbed over the side.

"I'm sorry about your necklace," it said. "I could retrieve it for you, if only you'd be so good as to give me a kiss in exchange."

"Odious frog," spat the princess. "Why must males of all species behave the same? Go back down your well and cease your talk of kisses."

"By your command," said the frog, and he turned and hopped back into the water.

Solveig continued on. If she could only find a city, she still had the circlet and the ring to sell. When she grew tired again, she slept, and when she woke, she trudged onward through the brush. By the following morning, the thick trees and tangled brush gave way to tall, swaying grasses peppered with wildflowers under a bright blue sky. Still there no city in sight, but near the edge of the forest, she had found some bramble berries and even an apple tree to sate her hunger.

After walking most of the day through the open fields, she came upon a vast lake. Although she had rinsed her face in the well the previous day, after two days and nights of traveling and sleeping in the dirt, a proper soak would be most welcome. She removed her gown and wrapped the diamond circlet in the fabric, and then waded into the reeds in her shift.

The cool water felt good on her skin, and after scrubbing off as much of the grime as she could, she paddled out towards the center where the water was so deep she could no longer touch the bottom. There, she floated and dove and did flips then paddled around some more. For the first time in her life, she could swim as long as she wanted, laugh as loudly as she wanted, and nobody was around to shush her or tell her to behave herself.

When she grew tired, she swam back to shore and by the time she had dried off enough to put her gown back on, it was getting dark. As she pulled the thick fabric over her head, she noticed that her emerald ring was missing. It must have fallen off her finger while she was swimming.

"Bother," she muttered to herself. She had no idea when she'd lost the ring. It could be over in the reeds where she might find it again if it didn't get too buried in the muck at the bottom, but she remembered seeing it on her finger while she was scrubbing herself. It seemed more likely to have fallen off while she played around in the deeper water.

Sighing to herself, she picked up her circlet and placed it firmly atop her head. Surely this would still sell for enough to get a room and something to eat besides berries and apples. As she turned to leave, a familiar voice called out to her.

"Hello again, princess."

It was the frog. He was floating amid the reeds, his long back legs stretched out behind him. "I believe I saw your ring glinting in the mud somewhere around the center of the lake. Would you like me to get it for you? I'd be most happy to."

Solveig narrowed her eyes. "At what cost?"

The frog pumped his legs once, darting closer to her. "All I ask in return is a single kiss."

"In that case," she said, "no thank you." She turned on her heel and strode away from the lake. When it grew too dark to continue, she lay down in a patch of soft grass.

"Odious frog," she muttered to herself as she closed her eyes to sleep.

The next morning, Solveig continued her journey. As the day wore on with no sign of a city, town, or even a passing merchant, she began to hope for more berry bushes or even a patch of bitter wild onions. Her stomach twisted itself into knots, growling and groaning so loudly she was tempted to eat a few of the wildflowers just to take the edge off. Unfortunately, the only flowers she knew to be edible were dandelions, and so far, the only ones she found had already turned into fluffy orbs. By mid-day, she hadn't found anything to eat, so when she reached a river, she decided to stop and try to catch a fish.

Having never fished before – it being unladylike and quite unbecoming for a princess – she wasn't quite sure what to expect from the experience. However, she did know that fishing required a pole and a hook and some string, and she of course had none of those things. But she remembered hearing tales of people catching fish with their bare hands in some sort of tournament game. Since her hands were the only tools she had available, she decided to give it a try.

As it turned out, catching fish by hand was a lot harder than she would've guessed. After nearly an hour of creeping up and plunging her hands into the water, all she had to show for it was a sopping wet gown and a bruise on one knee where she'd slipped on a rock.

She flopped down on the riverbank, exhausted, disgruntled, and still very hungry. A short while later, a familiar frog hopped onto a nearby rock.

"Why are you following me?" Solveig demanded.

"We frogs are natural fishers," he said, ignoring her question. "I could help you catch something to eat."

"Go away, odious frog," she replied. "I have no interest in your talk of exchanging kisses for favors."

"By your command," he said, but as he turned to hop from the rock, an enormous bird swooped down and snatched the frog in its beak.

Solveig jumped to her feet, pulled the diamond circlet from her head, and whacked the bird with it as hard as she could. It squawked indignantly, released the frog, and flew off.

The frog sat very still for a long moment, during which he regarded the princess with a look of great puzzlement.

"Are you all right?" she asked.

"You saved me," the frog replied. "That bird tried to swallow me and you smacked it without a second thought. Why would you do that?"

Solveig shrugged. "If I were about to be eaten alive, I would prefer that anyone looking on might do the same for me."

The frog sat quietly for a little longer and then hung his head.

"I have been an odious frog," he admitted. "All this time, I've been trying to bribe you for a kiss and refusing to help when you didn't agree. Then a bird tries to eat me, and you save my life without a moment's hesitation. I'm truly sorry, princess. If you like, we can go back and retrieve your ring and your necklace."

"I can't go back," she said. "There's still a chance my father sent his hunters after me, and I've no wish to be captured and sent home. But

I'll forgive you as long as you promise not to do it again."

"Agreed," the frog said with a mighty croak. As he said this, a warm golden light surrounded him and lifted him into the air. The princess looked on with wide eyes while his webbed feet morphed into fingers and toes, his slimy, green skin turned pale and grew hair, and his frog snout became a nose and lips. Once transformed, the light bathing him dissipated, and a young man with bright green eyes stood on the rock.

"It's broken," he said, flexing his fingers and hopping from one foot to the other. "The curse is broken, princess!"

Solveig, who realized her heart had been pounding at the sight of true magic, forced herself to close her mouth as she averted her eyes. Whatever magic had transformed the frog into a man had not been able to give him clothes, and the sight of him hopping about was almost as startling as the magic itself.

"I'm happy for you," she said, staring very pointedly at a dragonfly perched on the riverbank. "I never would have guessed you were truly human under all that slime."

He laughed and hopped off the rock. "I wouldn't be if it weren't for your assistance!" He approached Solveig and knelt in the grass next to her. "My lady, I'm a prince from a distant land, and now that I'm restored to my human form, I shall return home to claim my birthright. I would be honored to have one such as you as my queen and I vow to spend the rest of our days repaying you for your kindness."

Solveig allowed herself to meet his eyes and gave a small smile. "I thank you for your offer," she said. "But I've really no interest in princes or kingdoms any longer. If you wish to repay me, merely point me in the direction of the nearest city, that I might begin to make a life of my own."

The prince rose to his feet, a look of utter perplexion on his face. "If that is your wish," he said slowly, as though he couldn't believe the words were being spoken aloud or that he might be the one saying them. "If you follow this river upstream at a steady pace, you'll reach the city of Frihet before sundown. It's a modest city, but a lady such as yourself should have no trouble finding accommodations."

"You have my gratitude, frog prince," she replied, also coming to her feet. "I hope you find happiness when you return to your kingdom."

With that, she turned and followed the river upstream, and as the prince had promised, she reached Frihet before the sun began to set. There, she sold her diamond circlet to a duchess for far less than its value, but for more than enough to leave the life of Princess behind her and to begin her life as merely Solveig. Soon after, a group of hunters arrived in the city and inquired after a fair-haired maiden who may have been kidnapped by a band of brigands and would surely perish if she weren't located and returned to her worried father.

Solveig, whose hair was still fair, although considerably shorter than it used to be, had abandoned her heavy skirts for a pair of men's breeches and a belted tunic. She didn't hide when she heard the description being circulated. No one from her old life ever looked at her closely enough to recognize her now. Far more interesting were the tales of the cursed prince restored to his throne. The tales said he became a generous king and that his people prospered under his reign.

When news of his marriage reached Frihet, Solveig went down to the riverbank and caught a frog to have as a pet. She named it Odious and gave it kisses every time it croaked at her.

For the rest of her days, she lived – if not always happily – freely and with no regrets.

Stephanie Kraner *has been writing short stories alongside being a technical writer, blogger, and copyeditor for most of fifteen years. Her work has appeared in 200CCs, Anotherealm, flashquake, and others. She is not now, nor has she ever been, a dragon.*

Et In Vanadia Ego

Rosemary Sgroi

Jhon had already clocked up more units than he would need to pay for his journey but still he went flat out, full speed ahead. Approaching the station, he freewheeled down the ramp and onto the platform. A northbound Starley Express stood due to depart in eight minutes. In the second to last carriage from the end he found a vacant TronSpot, smoothly slid his bike up onto the grooves, connected his counter. Ignoring glances from fellow passengers to his left and right Jhon set about pedalling, head down, at the steepest resistance the TronSpot's rollers could muster. He was buzzing with a warmth that sprang not from these exertions, but from knowing that Maisry would be pleased he was on his way.

It had been the same with him for months. Every waking moment Jhon planned his next trip to Vanadia to see Maisry, pedalling almost constantly to max out his counter on the rollers at the office and at home. Most travellers worked, vidded or watched tubes while they accrued the bare minimum of units to cover the Starley fares. Those around him in the carriage now were waiting, settling themselves with drinks, connecting up devices before they began. But Jhon had brought nothing else to pass the time, only his bike and its precious cargo secured in a box on the rack.

The Starley slid away from the station through a vista of houses at first, then fields and sky passing in a blur. To him the rhythms of the pedals were fronds of colour, red and orange and yellow, flickering and sparkling, swirling, rising around Maisry as he pictured her waiting. The key thing was not to start worrying about what might go wrong once he arrived, and nothing helped but this: to keep his feet endlessly turning.

"Going far?" The man beside him had caught sight of the sum on Jhon's counter. He was maybe ten years older than Jhon, judging by his thinning hair and thickening adipose layers around the jowls and waist. Though wearing fully-vented hybridwear he was pedalling slowly at the lowest possible resistance, with regular pauses to sip a quart of PowerPro and to laugh out loud at something flickering on his vidder. It was one of the newest, slimmest models of multi-device with an integral counter, Jhon noted, though that was hardly a novelty anymore.

"Up north," said Jhon, declining to elaborate. Despite the recent completion of the new mainline, by which the northernmost isles could be reached in under six hours, few crossed the border these days. Long-distance travel to and from Vanadia had fallen sharply into decline since its independence from the rest of the union was formally declared. Complex entry tariffs, security checks, and the ever-rising cost of living in the north deterred all but the most persistent visitors from wanting to go there anymore. True, the Starleys that ran were packed, south of the border at least, but only because they were less frequent and had fewer carriages than Jhon remembered, back when the same journey used to take ten hours. Most of the passengers around him, he guessed, were commuters going no further than the next couple of stations.

"Never been north myself," the man said with a nasty chuckle. He was still staring at Jhon's counter. "Student, eh? Got a bitch of a loan to offload, I bet."

"Not anymore," replied Jhon. His gilet was emblazoned with the badge of Northern University, though he had never in fact been admitted there. It was second-hand, one of Maisry's attempts to help him blend in, to keep him alive as well as warm, she said. Otherwise he was indifferent to clothes, and so was she. That was one of the first things he liked about her. She saved her kWh for more important concerns than prissing about with appearances. There was no sense of performance in anything she did. The complete opposite of this uppish loser, Jhon thought. Something about the guy reminded him of Maisry's hateful brother, Marsh; but it was important not to think about Marsh, or any of her family, not now. He unzipped his gilet and stowed it on the rack behind his saddle in one smooth movement, without slackening the pace for more than a second.

"So what's your deal then, supercharger?" The man leaned forward, eye teeth bared in a mirthless smile full of latent aggression. His saccharine PowerPro breath and pungent aftershave cloyed the air between their TronSpots.

Jhon shrugged. Apart from what he spent on these visits, he quietly contributed most of his surplus to the grid and found it hard to understand the popular attitude of resentment towards anyone generating above their quota, as if it were some kind of effrontery. He wasn't trying to get rich or be a hero. All he wanted was to be left in peace.

"Drop it, Derrick," said a woman on the other side, without looking up from the tube she was watching.

But Derrick ignored her. He had ceased his own belaboured motion now, turning his attention wholly to Jhon's bike, which he appraised without comment until his eyes came to rest on the rack. "What's in the box?"

"For pity's sake, Derr, just leave the guy alone," the woman repeated, echoing Jhon's thoughts. Raising the volume of her vidder she began gyrating her arms as well as legs to the tinny jangling beat.

"It's empty," Jhon lied. He drew in a long breath and held it. Despite the open vents the carriage was thick with the stench of sweat, fast food, and something sour, a foul, furred taste in the air.

"Huh, so you can load it up with solid bars of vanadium," said Derrick. He had the attention of the entire carriage by now. Jhon could tell everyone was listening, even those who were still vidding or else pretending to be busy. One or two had ground to a halt while they waited to see what would happen.

But Jhon paid no heed. Pumping powerful quads, flexing taut, sinuous calves, he fixed his eyes on his faithful, familiar bike: a good one, old but reliable. On it he had generated more kWh so far this year than some made in a decade, though not of course enough to buy much vanadium, the battery component discovered and mined in the north that had made the whole grid system possible. The mega-rich owner of the TronSpot franchise supposedly rode a custom-built bike with a vanadium-alloy frame; a dumb kind of gimmick for the sake of notoriety, typical of a northerner. To most people there was little incentive to pedal more than the minimum required to pay their contribs and meet their own immediate energy needs. But since the north splintered off from the rest of the union, there was no knowing how many extra units his next trip to see Maisry might cost. Without looking up he straightened his back for a moment, rolled his shoulders, before continuing as before.

Soon after they first met, back when they were both in graduate school, Maisry had left a piece of paper clipped under the rack of his bike, on the railings outside the library. A handwritten note inviting him to meet her for lunch. No vidcode to reply to, no choice but to go. Many of the bike's components had been replaced since then; brake pads, a spoke or two, the chain more than once, saddle, even the handlebars, but never that old rack. He smiled to himself at the thought; they were barely more than children in those carefree college days. His memories seemed more real than anything that had happened since Maisry transferred to Northern, sacrificing so much to return to her family; and once he started work, years of travelling to visit her secretly there as often as he dared had passed in a blur by comparison.

The Starley was slowing. Through the window Jhon glimpsed the looping cycloducts and highrises of Midway as passengers around him began to gather themselves to descend. Again, though it was customary to cease pedalling while the Starley was stationary, Jhon kept on going, eyes half-closed, in a world of his own.

Before he knew what was happening his counter was gone. The chirp of the disconnected TronSpot sensor was almost drowned out by the bustle of passengers and their bikes vacating or filling the few available slots. No one else had seen anything, nobody realized he had been robbed. Frantically he looked around. Derrick and the woman were nowhere to be seen. The carriage doors were closing. Jhon had no chance to unhook his bike in time to get off.

The Starley was already pulling out of the station, the city smoothly fading into the distance, when he found the alarm lever.

"So it was stolen just now, at the station?" The inspector scratched away at his screen with maddening deliberation. "What model was the device, did you say?"

"Just a basic counter with a lot of units; over twelve thousand kWh. A bloke next to me kept going on about it. His name was Derrick and he got off at Midway," said Jhon, only becoming aware as he heard himself of how pathetic that sounded.

"You saw him take your counter?"

"No, but he wouldn't leave me alone."

"And what did Midway station security say?"

"I couldn't report it, I don't have any other device," said Jhon, with growing frustration. "I have no means of paying for this journey now, or the return fare."

The inspector seemed bemused. Theft of counters was rare, almost unheard-of; units could not be transferred between accounts except in very particular circumstances, and the biometrics were supposedly too sophisticated to be hacked. "Where did you say you were going?"

"Up north." Jhon had not given his destination, guessing in advance the likely response.

With raised eyebrows the inspector put through a message and repeated the information over to the city police, then vidded the station while Jhon stood by.

"What you should do is get down at the next stop, go back to Midway and see if it's been handed in at the lost property booth. Probably this is all just some kind of mistake, or a prank. You could try vidding your friend Derrick, too; maybe he'll be able to help you." The inspector slid his screen into a pocket and was about to leave when he turned back, pointing a finger in Jhon's direction. "The levers are for emergencies only. Heart attacks, that sort of thing. Really I should fine you for improper use, five hundred units."

"All my units were on my counter, as I told you." Jhon's voice crackled in despair. "I don't have any other devices."

"Well, you have been warned." The inspector tapped his bulging pocket and went on his way, whistling tunelessly.

Alone, standing beside his bike as passengers pedalled all around him intent upon their vidders, Jhon found his legs were shaking, though whether from rage or unaccustomed inactivity he could hardly tell. He ate a calorie bloc, swigging sap from his holster, without tasting either.

If he crossed the border without a counter he might not be allowed to re-enter the country. The inspector was right, he should get off; except it would all take too long, far more time than he could spare. Turning back now, whether he found the counter or not, would force him to postpone the whole trip for months until he could justify another leave of absence from work. Worse than losing his units was the wasted chance after so much meticulous planning. In every fibre of his body all he wanted was to reach Maisry, to press on regardless and complete what he had set out to do. Seeing the box still safely attached to his rack he crumpled, shoulders silently heaving.

Another passenger, a grey-haired woman who had silently observed Jhon's exchanges first with Derrick and then the inspector, crossed the carriage and held out a clean handkerchief. She rested her hand on his back briefly, a branding iron searing through his thin shirt, until after an awkward moment she patted his shoulder and went back to her TronSpot.

The Starley slowed, approaching the next station, and halted. Amid the influx of travellers looking for free spaces, Jhon remounted his bike, unconnected as it was, and ignoring their stares he started to pedal.

He would rather be stranded in the north and starve, he decided wildly, than return home now. On his previous visits he had found northerners hostile and backward-thinking, as was perhaps to be expected in the world's last outpost of capitalism, but he would just have to get used to that and so much else. There were greys, flinty and metallic, great choking clouds of doom in his mind's eye now, but Maisry's face was clearer somehow than before.

Almost three hours going through border control, and another hour and a half to wait before confirmation came through on the crossing official's vidder that no counter registered in Jhon's name had been handed in at Midway or any other mainline station. He was bound over to pay outward and return fares, border fees and surcharges, and issued with a temporary replacement counter after submitting himself to thorough scanning for a further couple of hours.

By the time he was free to go night had fallen. From hunger, tension, or both at once his stomach churned. The food and drink he had brought for the journey were long since consumed; the station shops were closed, and in any case he still had no units to convert into the old money they still used in the north.

Outside it was wet, desolate. As he fastened his gilet he shivered, wondering if the border authorities had only given him the benefit of the doubt because he was wearing NU insignia. The rest of his life had receded into a distant nothing, left far away.

What he had come to do he might as well get on with, now or never. He glanced left, right, and behind, not expecting to see Maisry's brother Marsh, but nervous nevertheless. Marsh, who had sworn to kill Jhon, to grind his bones and eat them. For no other cause than not being a northerner.

Slowly and wearily Jhon toiled up the long, steep climb into a cutting headwind. After so many years using the broad, neon-lit, perspex-covered cycloducts that criss-crossed most major urban areas, he had grown unaccustomed to riding in darkness, let alone this exposure to wind and rain.

With leaden legs he dismounted and unclipped the box, carried it tenderly along dim, stone-strewn paths until he came to the place, a spring at the head of an underground stream. There was a lot to be done. He was trespassing on their land but Jhon could only hope neither Marsh nor any of Maisry's family had been up here since his preceding visit, or indeed since she died at their hands, burnt alive for refusing to renounce him. It was heartening to think they had no idea of what he was creating here, for her. He cleared away moss, cut back weeds and grass, and began to dig.

Out of the box at last came the spliced botanical, a work of living art he had toiled over in secret for months, raising dozens of saplings until he found the right combination, the right colours, the weave to grow into Maisry's statue. If he set up each part correctly they would fuse in time with her charred bones and the other carefully sculpted pieces he had brought on previous occasions. Smudging his eyes on his sleeve from time to time, he laboured until birdsong announced the dawn, making everything perfect in ways he thought were sure to bring her lasting happiness. It would become an eternal memorial, growing stronger and more beautiful with every ray of light and drop of rain.

At sunrise, his task at last accomplished, Jhon knelt and rinsed his fingers in the icy trickle of the spring, holding fast to one thought alone, of his Maisry in paradise.

Rosemary Sgroi was an academic historian before taking up creative writing. Based in Coventry, she was selected for the Writing West Midlands 'Room 204' programme in 2017/18. Her main work in progress is a novel set in sixteenth-century England. *https://rosemarysgroi.weebly.com/*

Little Escher

Robert Borski

As I note in the introduction to my son's first book, despite my days as a civil engineer, I have little talent for drawing; thus if there's a genetic component to Jamison's artistic abilities, it has not come from me. But even as an adult, I can still remember the endless hours of pleasure drawing used to provide me as a child, splayed out on the floor with a box of broken crayons and numerous drafts of army tanks being strafed by jet fighters or cavemen fighting off legions of dinosaurs. And so while I wait for my son to be returned to me, of late, I've taken up his pencils and sketchbook, hoping as well to alleviate some of my anxiety and fears. In this one here, for example, you can probably tell which figure is Jamison, just by size alone (I'm hoping that he has grown some in the weeks since I've seen him last). The other figures -- cartoonish, I admit, but mostly what I'm drawing on for source material are movies and old plastic toys -- you can probably recognize for what they are, just as you can tell that this figure here, holding a weapon that is clearly not a ray gun, is me, the only adult in the picture, the one whose crude limbs are meant to represent arms and legs, not tentacles -- while all about us the alien spacecraft spins.

I can still remember, of course, the first time Jamison put a UFO in one of his drawings. We had just come back several months before from a grand tour of Europe (our second actually) and had spent the day at our publisher's, looking over a number of pre-publication details, including galley prints of the artwork. As usual, Jamison's sketches were fabulous and his bird's-eye views of Big Ben and the Eiffel Tower and the Coliseum were absolutely dizzying in their perspective and linework. Hugh Hollingsworth, our editor, no longer felt obligated to state the obvious by now -- how

nine-year old Jamison ("*a boy with no schooling or training...hell, not even the barest roots of a vocabulary...*") was able to produce his sketches simply by looking at the structure involved from the ground level, without access to any higher-up advantage -- but said simply, "No doubt Jamey here is a true phenom and this book will sell as well as the first three. Later, if you'd like, we can draw up a tentative schedule for the publicity tour. But in the meantime let me run another idea by you for your next book."

Jamison, of course, opaque to the conversation, sat fidgeting in his chair, looking down, kicking the chair's legs with indifference.

"Sadly, but momentously," Hugh began, flipping open a datebook, "we're coming up on the twenty-fifth anniversary of 9-11. And while we have a number of projects lined up already to commemorate the event -- mostly of a historical or political bent, or personal where-were-you- when- the-deal-went-down type reminiscence -- we'd like to offer something that paid tribute to old New York. By which I mean the one where the Twin Towers still dominated the skyline, along with all the other buildings that were destroyed at the complex."

"Er," I said, looking out the window in the direction of Lower Manhattan, "I can think of one immediate complication."

"Right. Right," agreed Hugh. "But we do have a number of alternatives. As you may or may not know, there's quite a detailed scale model of the World Trade Center right in the Museum. We could also possibly do a larger mock-up, maybe even utilize holograms or CGI to bolster the illusion. Our question to you: do you think that without recourse to the actual physical property or original structures, Jamey could produce the type of drawings he's renowned for?"

I thought it over a bit, looking at my mute

cowlicked son. "Only one way to find out, I guess."

Typically, when asked about the type of child they would like to have, prospective parents will say something like *the healthy kind, with ten fingers and ten toes*. Jamison, born digitally sound, had other problems however, although it took us almost a year-and-a-half before we realized this. Up until then Angela and I thought we had a normal bouncing baby boy; only later, after reviewing footage from our endless rounds of camcorder video were we able to have therapists point out to us what were clearly signs of Jamison's disorder (he never smiled nor babbled, fussed when he was picked up, never ever said *ma* or *da*). The usual guilt and recriminations followed; Angela -- a formerly heavy smoker, but who'd smoked a total of only three cigarettes during her entire pregnancy -- blamed herself for a while, until she saw on ladies' daytime television a program that steadfastly maintained childhood vaccinations were responsible. It did not matter to her that Jamison's problems were well documented before we ever took our son in for his DPT shots. She also began to spend more and more on-line time with fringe groups that advocated either prayer or holistic medicine could restore our son's "stolen" health, especially if you purchased their designer supplements. But to her credit she did join with me a community support group for families with children like ours. It was several years later, shortly after our divorce, that the group was first contacted by a university research team looking to assess savant abilities in cognitively-remote children. Given that I had an old electronic Yamaha keyboard at home that I played from time to time and he had no more taken to than he had to talking or social interaction, I thought Jameson an unlikely savant, but apparently there were other areas besides music that the university tested for. I must admit I was also unimpressed when Project Director Rhadha Singh came to me with a series of drawings I interpreted as little more than childish squiggles. "You don't understand, Mr. Rowe," she immediately countered. "Your son is four. His manual dexterity is extremely limited. But these pictures, while crude and somewhat simplistic, depict not only a playground with all the equipment proportionately sized and placed, but how that playground looks from forty feet up. Do you know what that means?"

"That my son has eyes on the top of his head?" I quipped. "That he can fly?"

"No, silly," she chided, wagging a dark finger in my face. "It means your son can rotate, examine, and depict three dimensional objects in space. But without ever actually seeing things in the real world from that perspective."

And that was the beginning.

When it comes to what Jamison does best, I would like to say that a kind of rapture comes over him and you can see glints of the occult intelligence within, the latent part of his brain that takes over whenever he sees something he wishes to draw, releasing his inner Leonardo da Vinci. To be sure, he does look enough like a regulation small boy, with tow-colored hair and Angie's brown eyes, and almost always perpetually untied shoes. (Despite the fact he can manipulate in his mind massively complex knots -- topological structures, according to Dr. Rhadha -- and depict what they will look like from any angle, he still cannot, or won't, tie his laces, nor wear slip-ons.) But it's here, in fact, where his aspect and affect look most flattened, devoid of emotion or anything remotely beatific, and from previous experience I knew not to disturb him or risk a true storm of emotions. Unlike most other artists as well, once Jamison begins, he never looks up again at what he's depicting for additional visual reference, but instead proceeds until he is done, even if it takes as long as several hours. The one compensation: more often than not, when finished, it's here that my damaged child will submit to a hug or small endearment --

moments too far and few between in my experience, but which I would gladly not trade for however many weeks on the best selling lists.

As for that future project of Hugh's and the money it would potentially earn, we'd already encountered one potent stumbling block: upon approaching the long lines queuing outside to enter the National Memorial, Jamison had become entranced with the Freedom Tower. Not that I blamed him; with its prismatic height and chamfered corners, it looked like the sort of gnomon his favorite artist would design, presenting two different looks, depending on where you stood (rectangular vs. sloped and twisting, box vs. braid).

"No, no," I tried arguing. "Come on, son. We're going inside first. Mr. Hollingsworth wants you to draw him a pretty picture of something that's really neat in the Museum."

But it was already too late. Jamison had already taken out his pencils and tablet from his backpack and had begun to sketch.

Shrugging, I turned to Hugh. "Maybe after he's done, he'll consent to do a second one right away. It's happened before."

"Not a problem," said Hugh, with a broad smile of bonhomie. "No reason we can't include before-and-after pictures. No problem at all."

The next half hour proceeded in much the manner of every other one of Jamison's non-restricted drawing sessions. Eventually, he was noticed and recognized, and you could hear various remarks from the strolling visitors, quite a few members of which did the crane and look-see, trying to cadge a view of his artwork.

"Hey, isn't that the kid who was on *60 Minutes*? The artistic savant -- you know,

retarded at the same time?"

"Yeah. Yeah. What's his name again? 'Little Escher'?"

But overall, as befitted the venue, a somber mood prevailed, and it was hard not to be moved by both the grandeur of the Memorial and the gravitas of those emerging from the Pavilion, many of whom still had wet eyes. I myself was thinking about where I was that fateful Tuesday morning and my own incredulous reaction when the announcement was made over our high school intercom. But then suddenly I felt a tug on my arm: it was Jamison, holding up his completed picture.

"Show Mr. Hollingsworth, son," I said, content just to listen there for a moment to the sound of the wind in the oak trees and the two nearby waterfalls.

"Something I don't understand, Ted," Hugh said shortly. "Not that the picture isn't strikingly done, despite the unusual straight-on perspective. I've never seen Jamey do that before. But --" frowning, shading his eyes with his hand, looking up into the midday sun" -- what the deuce is this supposed to be?"

And that's when we saw it for the first time -- the giant silver craft floating like a cloud high above the Freedom Tower obelisk -- the spaceship which existed only on paper, not in the real world. My son's very first demonstration at age nine that he had something akin to imagination or artistic license.

To identify location in the second picture I've been working on, I put a sampler on the wall that reads *Home Sweet Home*. Jamison and I are both there, of course, and I stand between my frightened son and the two badge-wearing plainclothes government operatives. Currently, I'm debating whether I should add a series of word balloons to help indicate the nature of their visit and why they want to take Jamison away from me. Something to the effect of:

"If you love your country, Mr. Rowe, you will seriously consider our offer. At the same time you will be helping to further provide your son with the assets and skill-set he will need to survive in the outside world." (This will link to the primary agent speaking, the one whose red hair is cropped so short it looks like he's wearing a skullcap of blood.)

"He has a gift, sir." (This, then, the other -- he whose smell of cologne and testosterone I could still conjure up in my cell.) "You above all else should know this. And once his training's complete he can come spend alternate weekends with you."

"Right. After a few weeks at Pentagon Remedial, he'll be able to look at a satellite photograph and tell you if it's part of a nuclear enrichment facility. You might as well teach Puff-Puff here to write poetry."

(We have never had pets at Casa Rowe since the guinea pig incident, but trust me, the little four-legged creature in the picture with a tail is supposed to be a cat.)

"No doubt it will be difficult. We agree. But Dr. Singh assures us the boy can be taught with the right kind of curriculum and rigorous training."

Me, counter-arguing: "As well she should, given that her research grants are underwritten by the Defense Department."

A head-shake from Agent Blood, which I'll depict with motion lines. "Well, we're still hoping you'll reconsider, Mr. Rowe. But you do need to be aware, sir, we are prepared to do what we believe to be in the best interests of young Jamison here. And if that includes presenting a case to Social Services, so be it. We already have statements from Dr. Singh and the boy's mother, as well as a whole cadre of professionals willing to testify you are not only holding your son back, but that you're exploiting him for financial gain."

But by now, in the comic strip format I've been using to present my case, I'm running out of room. So instead of continuing -- I still have an hour before my lawyer shows up -- I decide to draw another picture. I could, of course, attempt to depict Jamison in his new environment, learning his ABCs and the Golden Rule, but instead I decide to draw a bunch of dinosaurs devouring an office full of social workers, at least one of which looks like my ex-wife.

The UFO, of course, stymies us. We are now back in Hugh's office after lunch, where Hugh is swallowing a handful of his post-prandial cholesterol-lowering meds. "You don't suppose this is supposed to represent one of the incoming jets, do you? I mean, is that even possible? That Jamey has some inkling -- either psychic or intuitive -- of what happened to the Two Towers back in 2001?"

"Well," I say, looking at the ellipsoid shape, executed in the softer lead of a B2 pencil (the rest of the picture is in dark F), "considering that everything Jamey usually draws is hyperrealistic, you can't really say it looks much like a jet. Or has any detail. And to tell you the truth, I'm not even sure he's ever been exposed to anything resembling a 9-11 documentary or discussion. Remember, we're talking about an event that took place a decade before he was born."

"On television perhaps?"

"Doesn't seem to care for it much," I say, watching Jamey kick his feet back and forth, letting his laces fly like miniature whips. "And when he does watch, he's just as intrigued by the golf or religious channels as he is by Nickelodeon or the Cartoon Network. Right, son?"

More fiddling. But these days I'm much less inclined to believe he's secretly working on some tenet of quantum theory in an arcane recess of his brain than he is simply abyss gazing. No longer does it occur to me to shake him into correctitude, or bemoan the fact he can solve a six-by-six Rubik's Cube (at least if Dr. Rhadha has not been feeding him Clever Hans subvocal clues), but fail to master basic shoe tying.

"You willing to give it another go at the Memorial tomorrow, Ted? I could put you up overnight at my place. We could work on the LE4 itinerary some."

"Might as well," I say, bending over to tie my son's shoes for the millionth time.

But the next morning Jamison wants nothing to do with drawing, even going so far as to throw his drawing materials to the ground, eliciting the disapproving stare of a security guard who comes over to see what the commotion is about. "Hey, little fellow," he says, once we explain the situation. "You behave yourself, hear? Show some respect." Then to Hugh, who apparently gives off more of a grandfatherly vibe than I do the parental equivalent. "Nice looking boy, considering. My condolences. He looks like a handful."

And so we thought that was the end of it. Whatever impulse or stimulus had caused Jamison to draw something that was patently not there -- I could posit you any number of causes, from electrocerebral static; to a latent glimmer of imagination; to an oncogenic bit of nacre -- now seemed operative no longer. And so we returned to Baltimore, to our normal routine.

Except that on tour a month later, doing a demo sketch for a network affiliate in downtown Dallas, the UFO appeared again. Ditto for Jerusalem on the international leg. Then double ditto, this time while touring Japan -- for a total of four more.

Whether at this late date there will be more -- or even drawings where there's nothing but the simple glories of human architecture -- depends on who has my son and how soon (I refuse to think *if*) he's returned to me.

Unfortunately, my lawyer has more bad news for me -- that Hugh Hollingsworth is still suffering from the effects of his stroke and hence will be unavailable to testify or be deposed until (fingers crossed) his aphasia resolves. He also continues to advise me not to submit to a lie detector test since the results will be inadmissible in court. I further badger him to tell me if what my cellmate has heard from his daughter is true -- that I am being excoriated on local talk radio, where hardly anyone believes my story about how masked intruders broke in and kidnapped my son (at least I think they were masked; it was dark and it seems to me real aliens would look a little less rubbery); while still others maintain that I am the source of the UFOs in Jamison's renderings, added after completion to further hype and therefore boost sales. Finally we discuss how I will plead tomorrow at the preliminary hearing and I am told once more by my obsequious lawyer how he truly believes I am innocent.

Sleep, however, eludes me later. So out comes the drawing tablet. But what shall I draw this time? I've never much cottoned to the time travel theory -- that somehow, defective though the prism of Jamison's brain might be, he could make out these mysterious craft, filled with sightseers intent on revisiting 9-11 or the JFK assassination, the decimation of Hiroshima and Nagasaki, the Crucifixion. Why would they want to kidnap an inarticulate witness to their jaunts? To supersede any possible butterfly effect? I don't buy it. Nor do I much favor the alien visitors angle, although much to my surprise Angie and her cultmates have not dismissed the idea entirely; then again they think the late Art Bell was both prophet and messiah. So what, then?

In the end I decide to work a little on the picture I've been drawing of Jamison and me. It's actually a sketch-over, using as a backdrop M.C. Escher's 1953 Lithograph, *Relativity* -- a facsimile of which we've always included as a frontispiece in each of the *Little Escher* books and that Jamison has spent entire days staring at. In order to make us stand out from the other sixteen figures ascending or descending, I've used a darker shade of graphite. This small figure here -- the one pulling himself up by his bootstraps and meant to initially represent my son -- I'll probably erase. Instead I'm going to place him on one of the gravity-defying stairs and me on another.

Hopefully, along the way, before father or son meet in any hypothetical middle, neither will fall off or float free.

.

.

Robert Borski lives in Stevens Point, Wisconsin. He has been previously published in Analog, Asimov's, F&SF, and Strange Horizons, and two volumes of his poetry (BLOOD WALLAH, CARPE NOCTEM) remain available.

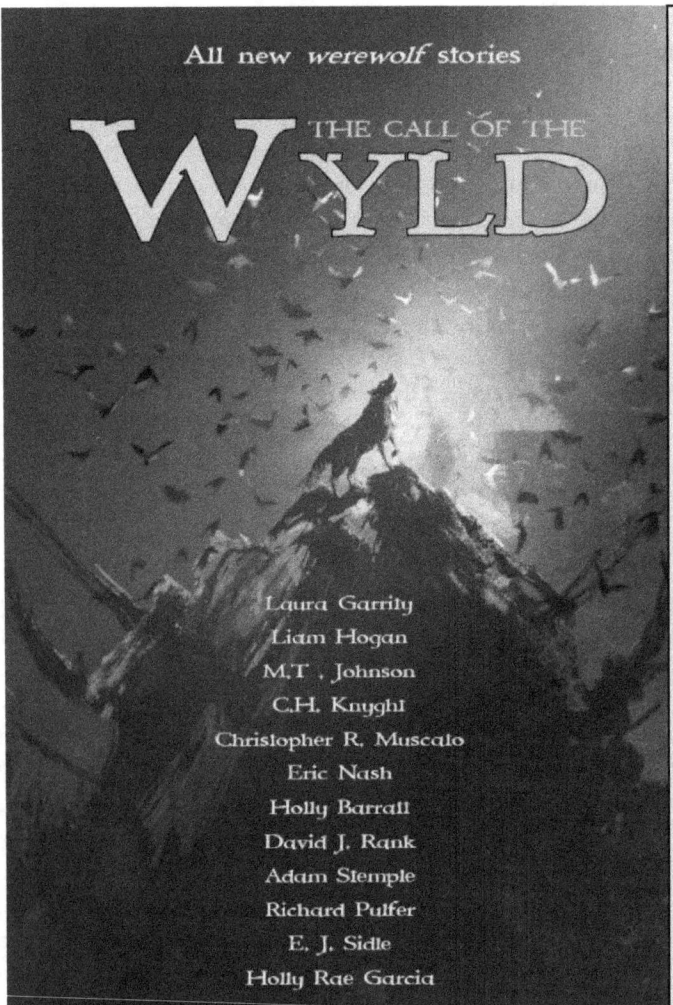

A Murder of Crows

Jacey Bedford

She stood on the rooftop parapet, staring through oily rain at the heads-down pedestrians scurrying five storeys below; all black in the slick neon-spiked darkness, even to her sharp eyes. She folded her arms across her chest, left hand fingering the rough threads on her right sleeve where her badge used to be.

"Anka, come inside. You've only been home four hours. They said you had to take it easy."

She whipped her head round at the sound of Sledge's voice. Water sprayed from the ends of her rat-tail hair and dripped down the neck of her leather great-coat. One annoying drop ran down her back and a second trickled between her breasts.

"Have you been practising or am I getting careless in my old age?"

"You're twenty-seven."

"Older than I deserve to be if I miss you sneaking up on me."

"Should I say you're a good teacher?"

She didn't want to be a teacher. Not again. One dead apprentice had been enough. One loss too many. She'd find some way to keep this overenthusiastic kid off the streets even if she didn't have a voice in the Department any more. He had no talent for it anyway. His enhancements hadn't taken. He should have been out of the programme by now.

He'd been so desperate not to fail.

While Illyn had been here Anka been able to put off the decision, but Sledge was first apprentice now. He couldn't hack it. Jasper should promote him to desk jockey. Keep him safe. How the hell he hadn't got himself killed while she'd been banged up, heartsick, in the evaluation centre, she'd never know.

"Come and look." She held out her hand to draw Sledge to the parapet. "I've missed all this." She drew a deep breath, taking in the city and its spaceport. "What can you see?"

Sledge shrugged. "Humans, Frecatons, Mirijis, a Stek or two. Hundreds of poor sods trying to make it home in the pissing rain without getting what passes for their brains beaten in or their belly ripped open by a maffi for the contents of their pockets. For pity's sake, come in, will you? I've got a skillet of fresh pancha on the hotspot. Don't make me eat them alone. You promised me weapons training tomorrow. It's been months since..."

"Tomorrow, yeah." She licked her lips. "But there's something going down tonight. I can taste it."

"It's not your watch. Let it go. Captain Jasper'll deal."

"Pah!" She pushed him away. "He can deal with the maffis. If it's a Crow incursion it's always my watch. I owe them."

I owe them for Illyn.

It wasn't over yet, no matter what Jasper said. No matter how many enquiries he stamped closed.

A double flash of unnatural rose-white light strafed the street below and was gone in an instant, leaving Anka with a visual imprint of hundreds of startled faces, human and non-human, frozen in the moment. A light bomb and probably a low level, localised EM pulse, too. She tasted the heavy air. Yes, definitely.

People began to hurry about their business, even the few small groups of Steks, whose sensory organs didn't include eyes. It was as if they'd felt it. Maybe they had; who knew how a Stek's senses worked.

Low-frequency sound rose through the building, via the soles of Anka's feet. It invaded her bones, and throbbed in the pit of her stomach. Crows.

"There! Feel it? I told you so." She half-turned, but Sledge had gone back to his pancha, too inexperienced to know where the duty roster ended and duty began. She considered calling him back, but he was safer here. Besides, her attention focused on darkness where there should have been light. The corner of Gunga Street and Nardini was a popular spot with thrill-seeking tourists for its Miriji bars and Freca native tat parlours. Instead of its usual blaze of ad-lights and aircart beams it was dark. Not just dark, but black. Unnatural black.

Crows!

"Sledge!" Anka ran six steps back across the rooftop to where she could see him in the garret, skillet in hand. "Stay put."

She turned and ran for the parapet, leaped onto the edge with one foot and over, free-falling four storeys and landing light as a bird, courtesy of spliced genes from her worst enemies. *Use their own against them.* She landed on the bakery roof and dived off, turning in mid air to splash down, feet-first into a puddle. An aircart honked and swerved, but she'd hit the ground running and was already gone from its lanespace. The part of her senses that monitored her surroundings for possible danger told her that people stared as she passed, but she judged them neither in danger not dangerous, so ignored them.

Three aircarts blocked the road ahead, their drives taken out by the pulse. The closest had already settled on its empty skirt, so she leaped on it, one foot on the engine cover, and pushed off for the next. It wobbled as she landed, not quite out of air yet. She adjusted her stride to completely clear the third, landing between an overturned delivery van and an abandoned caff-cart with water spigots still spitting steam from under its awning.

Blinking the rain away, she ran around abandoned vehicles and scurrying pedestrians. A low sound pulse thickened the air until it was like breasting a wall of water. Everyone she passed was running in the same direction—away—until the crowd thinned out to almost nothing. A Stek lay on the floor in a shapeless heap while another, a youngster, tugged at its left brachium, barely moving it. She skidded to a halt, gulping to stave off the nausea from the

subsonics. The Stek on the floor was either dead or completely comatose and about to die. Older ones were particularly susceptible to sound waves.

"You can't do anything, kid. Run or you'll get caught as well." She wrenched the youngster away, turned it round and propelled it towards

safety, hoping it understood basic. "Go!"

She began to run again, rounding the corner of Nardini and seeing the darkness up ahead, dense and menacing, squirming like a cloud of mini-twisters.

This was not the time to be stupid.

She slowed and scrubbed rain out of her eyes with wet hands, then stopped and listened, trying to tune out the subsonics. Up ahead in the darkness nothing else made a sound.

If it hadn't been for her keen hearing she'd have been caught. As it was she had barely half a second's warning before another light bomb blazed out. She flung herself backwards into a doorway and slapped both hands across her eyes. Even so she saw the bones of her hands illuminated against red flesh and felt the peculiar tingle that told her there had been another EM pulse. Good job she didn't rely on any implanted tech. Gods, she hoped Sledge had the sense to do as he was told. The kid thought he was ready for the streets, but he wasn't ready for this. Illyn *had* been ready and she'd still...

Somewhere close by a high pitched keening began and Anka saw a Frecaton female, her neck ruff fully fanned in agitation, stagger out of an alleyway ahead, drop to her knees and vomit. That was seriously bad. Frecaton emissions of any kind were not for the faint-hearted, especially when the throb of low frequency sound was already roiling in Anka's gut. The stench of the vomit reached her and she began to gag. She swallowed hard and closed her mind to the possibilities of throwing up. It could get her killed.

She thought of approaching the Frecaton, but this was their homeworld, and of all the species here they were the most resilient; besides, the Crows were almost certainly watching the street.

What did they want this time?

What did they always want? Some poor streetbait kid fresh out of the nursery? Whatever it was, she'd deal with it. That was what the Port Authority paid her for... Well, okay, right now she was on half-pay, but that was good enough.

She'd be less disturbed by their relentless kidnappings if she knew what happened to their victims, but once taken by the Crows they might as well never have existed. Slaves? Lunch? Sacrifices? Who knew?

Darkness was rare in the city, unnerving even without the fear that intensified as she got closer to the Crows. The streetlights glowed uselessly, giving off no light into the oily smog. Some kind of tech was swallowing light. It was tech.

Not magic.

Never magic.

She'd been to hell and back courtesy of the Crow King. Oh, gods, she could still feel his breath on her neck as he whispered his lies into her ear, but she still didn't believe in magic. The Crows used fear against people. It had to be tech, advanced enough so that no one knew how they did it; a low level telepathic field maybe; a neural net? How else could they generate that squirming, between-the-shoulder-blades, it's-behind-you feeling?

Nothing there. Trust your senses. She resisted the temptation to turn. *Don't get suckered in again.* Fear would eat you if you let it.

She'd tried to interrogate one of them once, a Crow female. They'd had a staring match for nearly eight hours before Jasper had called time and pulled her out. She'd been sedated for two days afterwards and Jasper had refused to tell her what they'd done with the Crow.

A low rumble to the east announced a shuttle lift-off. On the hour, every hour, day and night, some silver bullet blasted off either for the orbiting passenger stations or one of the mining bases on Echo, the second moon.

Out in Sector Five a siren wailed. Oh great, Jasper's finest were announcing their progress through the crippled streets. That gave her maybe six minutes to resolve this before they came rolling in for a smackdown, the kind of operation that got good people killed for no reason.

A brief vision flickered across Anka's consciousness: Illyn lying broken in a pool of her own blood one minute and consumed by Crow darkness the next,

A single gut-wrenching scream cut the air. The heavy, throbbing subsonics lifted. A silence flowed in thick in its wake. For a moment it seemed like the whole world listened; even the rain had stopped.

Anka ducked between the Gordy Tenement and Miskin's Fur Warehouse into a back alley. A wall of billowing black faced her, thick but odourless, leaving the foetid stink of the alley, piss, garbage and the lingering miasma of Frecaton. She took a deep breath, wrinkled her nose and tried to settle herself. She'd known a gentle darkness once, in a place far, far away, with a much sweeter aroma. The faint scent of woodsmoke and sage tickled the back of her memory. Her clan-mother's arms around her, warm and comforting.

Steady, don't get suckered. It isn't real; just another implanted meme.

She had neither mother nor clan. Move on.

She blinked, listening hard, feeling for heat sources.

Edging forwards, she made her way through the alley, stumbling twice, once over a grating, half unseated from its drain, and the second time over, well, best not think, but it had been dead long enough to have lost residual heat. Her foot scraped against something and the sound echoing back told her that the surrounding walls had opened out. She was in the delivery plaza behind a parade of shops and the Golden Platter restaurant.

"Who's out there?" A girl's voice, thin and high, cut the night. "They said you'd come... Please..."

She stopped and listened. Nothing but the girl, her breathing rapid and shallow. Fear.

"An... Anka. They said someone called Anka would come."

Anka felt her stomach muscles contract and a shiver run down her spine. If she'd had hackles they would have risen now.

"They've gone. If you can hear me. I'm tied up."

Following the sound of the girl's voice Anka skirted the plaza, sensing human body heat. A female, lying on the floor against the wall of the restaurant loading bay. There were no other heat sources, but it could still be a trap. She waited a little longer then edged closer.

"Is anyone out there?" The girl's voice was loud close up.

"Hush!" Anka said. And then checked all round again.

Nothing.

"Lie still." She crept to the girl's side.

"Anka. You're Anka, right? They gave me a message for you. They said... He said..."

As Anka's fumbling fingers found the tape round the girl's wrists they brushed against the soft vanes of a feather and the darkness around them dissolved. The bright sign hovering thirty metres above the restaurant splashed sickly yellow light on to the sodden ground and the rain began to fall again like spears, silver against the gold.

Anka hissed, drawing her fingers back from the glossy black Crow feather its shaft tucked into the sticky tape. Tape and feather fell to the ground and quickly became bedraggled gutter-trash.

"Are you hurt?" She went down on one knee, held the girl by the shoulders and drew her into a sitting position

The girl shook her head.

"That you screaming?"

"I never... I thought I was done for. What would you have done? I came out to dump the garbage and they caught me. I thought it was the maffi, thought my throat was going to get slit for sure. But it was Crows. Didn't do anything. Said I had to tell you..." She screwed up her eyes as if trying to get it right word for word. "Illyn is safe."

Anka hissed and let the girl fall back to the ground.

"Hey, no call to..."

"Liars!"

"I'm tellin..."

"Them not you. What else did they say?"

"Said you can come home whenever you want to."

"Bastards!"

"And..."

"Yes?"

"Sledge."

"What?"

"They named him *enemy*."

"No! No no no no no!" Anka leaped to her feet. Had all this been an elaborate charade to draw her away from Sledge? They'd killed Illyn. She'd seen her lying bloodied, still as death.

She'd disarmed the old man, bound him. She was sure. Yet the Crow King spoke and the shackles dropped away. And Illyn had fallen...

If technology was advanced enough it looked like magic.

It was tech they had. It had to be tech.

Didn't it?

First Illyn and now Sledge. Gods, he was off duty. Cooking pancha. Not expecting trouble. Couldn't handle trouble by himself if it was delivered to him trussed up in a basket.

Leaving the girl on the wet ground Anka turned towards home and ran. Back down the alley, through the mess of slewed vehicles and dazed people. Jasper's squaddies were already spreading out across the square. No time to deal with Jasper now. She dropped to a walk and they didn't even spot her. No wonder Jasper needed streetbait like her and Illyn and, if he ever made the grade, Sledge. They were all that stood between the city and the Crows.

Once clear of Jasper's boys she dropped her head and raced down the street again. The Stek that the kid had been trying to revive was obviously dead. Gods, they decomposed fast. She tried not to breathe as she bolted past it.

Anka shared her cheap rooftop apartment with her apprentices, just Sledge now because she hadn't had the heart to fill Illyn's empty place.

He's only eighteen, only eighteen, she kept saying to herself over and over again like a mantra as rain streamed down her face like tears. She slowed as she neared the last corner, checking ahead for telltale darkness. Nothing. She tucked into the wall of the grocery store across from the bakery and stared up.

Apprentices! More trouble than they were worth. You got too involved. Started to care too much. Hung on to them because they were all the family you were ever likely to have. Ruik had it right. Her nursery sib had refused apprentices right from the start.

She didn't used to worry, but since she'd found the streetbait nursery. It bothered her that foundlings were used like that. It seemed different looking in from the outside. It hadn't bothered her half so much when she was going through it herself. The enhancement surgery, gene therapy and mental conditioning seemed normal.

She wasn't supposed to remember the nursery, but after that first close encounter with the Crow King she'd had questions about her origins. Big questions. It took a diligent shakedown of the files to get the first clue, but she'd eventually found the place, seen the kids, calm faces, livid surgery scars, thousand metre stares. It made her flesh creep to think she'd once been like them.

They grew into smart kids, but how many of them lived past thirty? Her own cradle-sibs, Ruik included, were all dead. At twenty-seven she was almost a legend, the only known survivor of a Crow snatch.

As if a tap had been turned off the rain stopped. The night air smelled faintly fresh before the city scents flooded back, wet garbage, Frecaton and... fried pancha. Sledge's dinner. It was probably still hot. She craned her neck back to see, but the loft windows stared back, black and blind. Was she already too late?

Not daring to risk the doors she went straight up the side of the building, leaping to the bakery roof in a single jump, powering with both legs and stretching up with both arms reaching for the parapet and finding it easily, almost as if she had wings. Then she climbed, despite the wet, swinging from downspout to cornice and windowsill to cable anchor with ease. Flowing over the top parapet she dropped to a crouch, tucked into the low wall on the edge of their deck, a rooftop living space where they ate on fine nights and lazed on rare sunny days. A table and three mismatched chairs occupied the centre of the six metres between her and the double glass doors into the garret. This was the tallest building in the city segment, so no need for curtains. She could always see inside... but not now. A screen of darkness obscured the glass.

More Crow tech.

The back of her neck prickled and her mouth tasted of ashes.

The double doors opened and the lights blazed out. Silhouetted, hands on hips, bold and black against the yellow, stood the Crow

King, a long feathered cloak swinging softly to his ankles. The ancient enemy whose blood ran through her own veins.

Rage rose within her.

She'd been created to fight the Crows. Fight them to the ends of her being. They were merciless killers, thieves, abductors, torturers and, oh, gods, magicians.

"Anka." He held out both hands.

She unfurled herself and stood, calves against the outer parapet, five storeys of air at her back. Their element more than hers.

Her pulse pounded in her ears. No time to panic. She needed all her wits about her now or she wouldn't see the morning, and neither would Sledge.

"Anka!" Sledge's voice, inside the garret.

She started forwards, but the Crow King's hands changed from palms-up invitation to palms-out. Stop! She could barely move. It was like trying to breast the subsonics except there were no sound pulses. She took one painful step.

"Interesting." The Crow King's voice, deep and resonant, brought back whispered words to her mind. Words she didn't want to remember.

You are of us. You will return to us.

"Let him go!" She spat the words out.

"Soon."

For three breaths neither of them spoke and then the Crow King stepped forwards, pulled a chair out from the table, sat on it and leaned back casually. Behind him she could see half a dozen Crows. Two held Sledge in an arm-lock, down on his knees, head bent forward. Another straddled his feet and stood behind with a hand on the back of his neck. It looked like a still from an execution scene.

"Sit." The Crow King snapped his fingers and kicked a chair in her direction. The thick air released her.

She sat. In the outspilling light the Crow King's blue-black skin was as firm as good leather, tight over high cheekbones where the feather-vanes began and swept backwards up

and over his head in a hair-like cap, peaking down over his forehead between his bright eyes. Feathers covered his lean body. The black held an iridescence that spoke of hidden rainbows. In his own way he was glorious.

You are of us. You will return to us. His words echoed in her mind.

"Last time I gave you a choice," he said.

She dragged her eyes away from him.

"I made my choice. I came home."

"This is not your home."

"You're full of shit."

"You're not so sure about that as you once were, are you?"

"You killed at least one tonight." She pictured the Stek kid tugging at the brachium of its downed parent.

"Regrettable, but it was its time. We merely hastened it by a few hours or a few days at most."

"Like hell."

He shrugged. "This planet is ours. We will keep a portion of it whether humans like it or not."

In the distance the port threw up another shuttle with a dull roar that was so much a part of Anka's existence that she barely noticed it. The Crow King glanced up and scowled.

"This is the Frecaton homeworld," she said.

"Cattle. They were our cattle and we let them evolve to intelligence and have a life of their own. They sold mining rights which they did not own and so the humans came with their Stek miners, soon followed by Miriji traders and then--" His face twisted. "Tourists! They can have the moon, they can have the port, the city and its hinterland, but the wild is ours. We will fight to keep it." He leaned forward, forearms on the table. "And they can't have our children."

"I told you before..."

"But you went searching. You found the lab, saw for yourself. Found it for us."

"I found a genetics lab. Foundlings being enhanced, streetbait like me. Human children

48

with enhanced bones and a shot of Crow genes, all the better to stand against you."

"Crow children given human genes to tame them. Who else could hope to stand against us? Send against us soldiers that we will not kill."

"You've killed so many of us."

"Show me the bodies."

"Ruik."

"A knife from a maffi."

"Illyn."

"Safe and well."

"You say."

"Crows don't lie."

"Yeah?"

"Illyn..." He turned his head slightly. "She said you'd need to see her before you would believe."

A willowy Crow came to stand behind him, feathered head turned bird-like slightly to one side. Oh, gods, Illyn had always done that, right from her first day as an apprentice. But Illyn had been the colour of rich mahogany, not blue-black.

Could it be? Her face was the right shape, not pretty but beautiful; strong bones, hawk-like nose, round dark eyes.

Dare she let herself believe it? Was it some cruel trick?

"It's me, Anka. He's telling the truth. We only take back the stolen ones. And now we can get to the nursery." She pointed towards City Hall. "Jasper's known all along." She turned back. "Sledge knows."

"Sledge?"

"He's Jasper's spy."

"Even if I buy your story, Sledge is streetbait so doesn't that make him yours too?"

The Crow King stood. "See for yourself."

He led the way into Anka's own garret, the familiar cluttered room stuffed with comfortable possessions. A sagging couch covered with a faded throw, tech-terminal built in to the far wall with a direct line to Jasper. Counter and hotspot with the pancha pan pulled carelessly to one side and a sink full of pots.

And in the middle of the floor, still held firm between two Crows, Sledge.

"Don't listen to them, Anka. It's not her. You saw her die. You told me."

"I fell. I was injured," Illyn pushed her Crow cloak back behind her shoulders. "See. They healed me. They made me whole."

She held up her arms, but where there had been long, shiny scars on Illyn to match Anka's own her black skin was unblemished except for a row of tiny little buds.

"Benarot, he's a shaman, not only healed my bones, but he restored to me what was taken. I can fly, Anka."

The buds blossomed into quills which quickly grew into long, stiff, asymmetrically-shaped feathers along both limbs. She stretched out glossy wings and then folded them in again and in an instant once more had arms. Anka felt her mouth open but no speech came out.

"Tech. Some sort of tech."

Illyn laughed. "Call it what you will. Take off your coat. See for yourself."

Anka shivered. Never able to bear her arms being covered tightly, beneath her greatcoat she wore a sleeveless high-necked leather vest, pocketed for shackles, sidearm and badge, currently all in Jasper's desk drawer.

Illyn, if Illyn she was, stepped forwards and took Anka's left hand drawing her arm out level. "Feel."

Anka felt at her own scar with the fingertips of her right hand, feeling the tiny puckers spaced along it where quills might grow. "It's where they operated to strengthen our bones."

"No, it's where they clipped your wings. Feel the quill knobs."

The Crow King stepped forward. "Now feel at the boy's scars, nothing more than cosmetic. Lines on his skin. The bone is smooth"

"His enhancements didn't take properly."

"There never were any enhancements. They reduced you to less than you should be. Indoctrinated you. Altered you to look more like them, but left you with light, bones, strength, speed and endurance. Then they twisted you against your own kind with lies."

She started to deny it and then stopped.

The Crow King nodded and the two Crows holding Sledge hauled him to his feet and took him, whimpering to the edge of the parapet. "Tonight, Anka, you leapt from here and landed lightly. Even without wings you are a creature of the air. If I throw this boy over the edge will he fly?"

"Don't. Please. He may be the worst apprentice I ever had, but he's a good kid."

"Your Captain Jasper sent him here to watch over you. He's the worst apprentice you ever had because he's wholly human." The Crow King turned. "But you're not."

He nodded to someone behind her and she whipped round to see an old Crow man step out of nowhere. The same old man she'd shackled the last time she'd encountered Crows, when–if–Illyn had died.

"Benarot." The Crow King inclined his head. "Can it be done now?"

"The wings now. The rest later, if she survives."

"She'll survive. She's my girl." The Crow King touched her lightly on the shoulder.

Anka jerked erect at the fizz and snap of it.

He laughed. "And she knows it. She only needs to let herself believe." Then his face became serious. "This will hurt."

"Oh, yeah. I bet you're going to say it will hurt you more than it will hurt me."

"No. I just thought you might like a warning. It won't hurt me at all. Do it now, Benarot."

It started out as a tingle in her fingertips, then an itching and then her arms were on fire. Fire and cramps both at the same time, one bad and the other worse. The blinding pain stretched along her torso, into her breasts, ran along lines of muscle around her back then hit her spine and shot upwards into her skull and down the backs of her legs into her heels.

She must have fallen. Maybe she blacked out because when she knew herself again the pain was only a distant throb and she was huddled on the floor wrapped in feathered wings, her own.

"Come, child, stand." The old man knew just where to touch her to lift her to her feet. "You'll learn how to control the change for yourself and next time it won't hurt so much."

She raised one hand to her face, but she didn't have a hand any more. What felt like a hand had elongated to long narrow flight feathers which she could spread, separate and rotate, like fingers. Pinions, primaries, secondaries, tertials. She knew each feather for what it was.

Hers.

And it was a revelation. Somehow, even through the confusion in her brain, it felt right. She flapped her wings experimentally, feeling the potential lift.

"You'll need your tail feathers." The Crow King placed a feathered cloak around her shoulders.

"Do you think you can fly?" he asked.

"Fly?"

"There's only one way to find out."

She looked down. Jumping from the roof was something that had never worried her before, now it looked different.

"Look up, not down," Illyn said. "I was so scared the first time I had to do it."

"It really is you, isn't it?"

Illyn nodded.

Anka felt tears sting her eyes. A mixture of wonder and relief tinged with the kind of anger a parent feels when she's snatched a child's fingers away from a flame. "I grieved. Why didn't you...? I've missed you, dammit!"

Illyn smiled, teeth white against dark lips, a most unbirdlike expression. "I've missed you, too."

Then Illyn launched herself from the parapet. Her arms grew into graceful wings, her cloak formed a tail. She flapped three times for lift, turned on a wingtip and landed back down beside Anka.

"Your turn."

Anka teetered on the edge. The ground had never looked so far away before. Her wings altered her centre of balance, made her clumsy.

Illyn grinned. "Deep breath and step off. It's the only way."

The Crow King rested his hand on Illyn's shoulder, once more human in shape. "She will when she has a reason." He turned to Anka and slapped Sledge on the shoulder, knocking him to his knees on the parapet. "Anka, do you still say this man is genuine crow kin?"

"Let him go, please. He's only eighteen."

"I'm older than I look." Sledge's mouth twisted down at the corners, eyes hard. "I'd do it again in a heartbeat. I was trying to keep you from them--from the change. You all change in the end, if you don't die first." He shrugged. "But we get maybe six years of service out of you before you do. I thought you might be different. You were strong. Stubborn." He shrugged, suddenly boyish again. "And you liked my pancha."

"Please. I'll come with you." She flapped her wings in agitation and turned to the Crow King. "I don't really have much choice, do I? How could I explain these to Jasper? But let him go. I don't want him on my conscience, spy or not."

"He won't be on your conscience, he'll be on mine." The Crow King gave a sharp push.

Sledge toppled forwards in slowmo, arms flailing. No wings sprouted magically to save him. Without a thought for whether she could do it or not Anka leaped on to the parapet and pushed off. She swooped into Sledge's falling body and, lacking hands, wrapped her legs around him. He grasped her waist and buried his face in her breasts clutching convulsively, his fingers digging in. Gods he was heavy.

Her cloak moulded itself to her body and became tail feathers. She beat down with her wings, feathers on wing and tail generating both thrust and lift between them, working the air. She made a little height, but Sledge's weight dragged her back towards the unforgiving earth.

"Drop him, girl, he's going to kill you both."

The Crow King flew above, circling her. She felt the air currents as he passed.

"Sledge, let her go. I'll catch you," Illyn called.

But Sledge clung on.

Anka beat against the air with her wings again and again, but she was losing height fast. Too fast.

He was going to drag them both to their deaths. Her instinctive act of compassion was going to be her first and last as a Crow. She hadn't got enough air beneath her wings to recover and they were going to pile in to the street hard and fast.

Crows swooped to either side of her, guiding her, encouraging her. Illyn flew beneath her, taking some of Sledge's not inconsiderable weight to slow their descent.

"Down there. Not too close to the buildings," the Crow King ordered.

It was the plaza behind the Golden Platter, empty now.

Illyn dropped away. Anka could hardly hold Sledge. She smashed his feet into the floating Golden Platter sign as she came in over the rooftops, setting it rocking alarmingly.

Sledge yelled and began to lose his hold. Four metres above the ground she let go of him and made a recovery of sorts. She landed as if from a jump, folding her wings into her sides, keeping them tight furled.

Sledge rolled and came to a huddled stop, alternately cursing and whimpering, making no attempt to rise.

"Something's broken. My ankle, it's bloody broken. Ow!"

Anka knelt beside him. "You've got nerve, Sledge, I'll give you that."

She concentrated hard on having an arm again and fingers began to form instead of pinions. She hooked them under the badge on his sleeve, ripped it off and threw it down to the ground, then let her wing grow back. The Crow King landed lightly and turned the badge into molten slag with a word.

"Tell Jasper I resign."

"Get away from me." Sledge shuffled backwards then cried out and reached towards his ankle, not quite seeming to dare to touch it.

"Am I that scary, Sledge?"

She didn't know what she looked like any more. *Just the wings,* Benarot had said: <u>the rest later</u>. Maybe her skin was still brown, her hair still halfway human, but her wings weren't. She spread them now, like an avenging angel.

"Get behind a desk while you still can," she whispered.

She turned her back on him. "What about the rest of the streetbait?" Anka asked the Crow King. "And the nursery?"

"Our next call." He lowered his voice. "And when all our chicks are back in the nest the humans will have no leverage over us."

Another silver shuttle blasted skywards.

His voice hardened. "If the Port Authority wants to deal, the Frecaton High Council knows how to contact us," he said to Sledge. "They always have."

At his nod the black swirled in and Sledge whimpered. Anka steeled herself, but found it wasn't for her this time.

"You could have taken me any time. Why leave it this long?" Anka asked softly.

"We didn't know where the children were until you found them, and we didn't know you'd found them until we took Illyn."

"You could have got the children out two months ago."

"But we couldn't get you until today."

Did he care? That might take some getting used to.

"Ready?" he asked.

She nodded. "Is there a technique for this? Jump up and flap like hell?"

He laughed. "You'll get it."

She could try.

She jumped up and beat down with strong black wings.

Jacey Bedford writes fantasy and science fiction; she's been published on both sides of the Atlantic. Her first five books are published by DAW: **Empire of Dust, Crossways,** *and* **Nimbus, Psi-Tech** *novels. They are science fiction/space opera. Plus* **Winterwood, Silverwolf,** *and* **Rowankind (The Rowankind Trilogy)** *– historical fantasy set in 1800 with a cross-dressing female privateer captain, a jealous ghost and a wolf shapechanger. Her writing blog,* <u>Tales from the Typeface</u> *is on WordPress. You can follow her writing history from there as it happens; plus pick up writing advice and the writing-relevant minutiae of a writer's life.*

The Paint-Over Artist

Mark Rigney

Through the gate she went, not forgetting to duck the lowest of the pine's overhanging boughs. Step, step and step, up the short flagstone walk. Hand to latch, the door quick-tugged: inside in an instant, but the door would not be slammed, no, for Marta had made up her mind to be as placid as an evening pond. No histrionics, no tearful fidgeting, no extra noise. Even so, Avaun, test-tasting his latest voluminous stew, put down his ladle, licked his lips with a wince of it-needs-something, and said, "Marta. Talk to me."

A keenly observant man, Avaun, and such a good husband. All the women said so. Dutiful and strict, but fair with the children. Marta always returned from work to a hot meal, guaranteed. Not like some, women whose workdays ended in dragging their protesting, ne'er-do-well husbands from the nearest tavern.

On this night, resistance came first for Marta, long minutes' worth. Pieties and assurances, bromides. "No, no. It's fine. I'm fine. A beautiful day to be out and about."

But patient Avaun wouldn't accept her evasions, and time was not on his side, for the children were due back to their edge-of-the-city cottage quite soon. Net-craft: an after school class taught by Old Sesten. Knots and rope: like sewing, or loom-work, but no novice adult could keep up. No wonder Sesten loved to teach children, all of whom hoped with bated breath that this would be the day where their crusty instructor would let down his guard and tell a tale not of hooks, nets, or fishing, but of some grand contact on the faraway seas, some chance encounter with the *tathru*.

"Tell me," Avaun said, his voice firm, as she flopped across two chairs, draped as if glued there, never to shift again.

She said—such despond—"It won't go away."

"What won't go away?"

"It's only paint. So, it really can't do what it's doing."

Perhaps he would have learned more, but the children barged in (as even *tathru* children surely did), and so his probing ended. Marta ate sparingly, and he had to prompt her just to lift her spoon. "New combinations," he said, coaxing. "A true culinary experiment."

"My husband. Such the revolutionary."

Afterward she helped with the children, yes, tousling their hair and playing a losing round of jump-stones, but her smiles were rote, her attention scant. Avaun was glad when she went up early to bed. He tucked in both girls, Nilo first, then Thuma, and scrubbed down the kitchen. When a tubespy swooped close and hovered by the nearest window, peeking in, its wings (or whatever they were) thrumming, he slammed the shutters on it. Not in the mood! If he dared, he'd have downed it with his broom. He'd seen it done, witnessed with his own eyes the metals and who knew what all burst into shattered smithereens, but if he were to do the same? *Leave the tubespies be,* that was official policy. He might be jailed. Disappeared, even. At the least, he'd be hauled before the Broman.

Tired, Avaun fell into bed—too tired, really, to recall with any clarity his wife's bleak mood. His own day had been normal enough. All was well in hearth and home. He burrowed his face into Marta's hair, breathed her scent, and soon was fast asleep.

Next morning, Marta picked up her paint from the supply shed, prompt as always. After making sure the lid on the pail was tightly shut, she loaded it onto the department's rickety wooden handcart. Would the wheels last another day? That cotter pin didn't look up to the task, but what alternative did she have? She'd put in the request for repair weeks ago.

No more pins, they'd said. No more wheels, either. But not to worry, it's just a local shortage. Temporary.

She strapped the roller to the rails of the cart, then added the extension rod, extra roller heads, roller pans, mixing sticks, and rags. The fun part then: a broad selection of blue and violet pigments. D'Nan had said that there'd been at least four reports already that morning, all from the northwest quadrant. Northwest meant blue of one shade or another. No need for tawny tans, no need for reds or greens—although she often fancied changing a wall (or even an entire house) to an unexpected tint of her choosing. By the Broman's three great heads, some surely needed it! Indeed, it was a joke around the city that if it weren't for Municipal Beautification and Marta's all too frequent layers of patchwork paint, half the city's houses would have long since fallen down.

Northwest. Uphill. Dragging the cart was slow work, heavy work, but the city had hills, what could she do? Dig them down to level armed with nothing but her simmering anger (thirty years in the making) and maybe a shovel? No. One climbed the hills and took satisfaction that for every ascent, there'd be an easy downhill on the way home. Besides, the day was bright, sunny. No need to worry about rain ruining her work. This would be a good,

outside day, the kind that made her assigned duties something halfway close to...well. Not joyful, no. Tolerable?

Her real worry ran deeper, gnawing its way into all other thoughts: today, would the slogans stay covered?

Her destination was a private home facing Soldier's Square. Was this fine upstanding plaza more popular with pigeons or people? Impossible to say. The wall the vandals had chosen faced the square dead on, which was unfortunate. The bastards were getting bolder, no question. Not that this would be a complicated repaint, despite the three upper-story windows. Every last letter of the slogan ("Dare to Be Skeptical") was well below their sills.

Test batches of paint, that was next; a swatch here, a swatch there; get it to where a normal eye would never see the difference.

Unless...

Stop it, she told herself, as the morning crier made an appearance by the plaza's derelict, cracked fountain. There was no "unless."

The crier, not one she recognized, seemed not to have memorized her news at all. The crowd that gathered to hear shifted like disquieted sheep, and one or two plaza windows shut with deliberate bangs. Marta listened with half an ear to the jerky, unpracticed weather forecast and the generic reports of crops and catches, generic in that they were glowing, simply reeking with steady, organized optimism. The Broman loves you all, my friends. Your servant the Broman loves you all!

The one interesting bit—stutter-stumble, hesitate-um, this crier truly was pathetic—came at the end. A rescue at sea, a *tathru* ship adrift and foundering in the wake of a storm. Salvage operations had commenced overnight, for the

Bromans were merciful, as always. The *tathru* survivors will be held on the islands, on the outermost islands, rocks and gulls, gulls and rocks. Have no fear, good citizens! No Broman would ever endanger you by bringing them ashore. And as for our people engaged in the operation, stay calm (stumble hesitate): there will be no contamination. All those involved will be secluded (for their own good), processed with care, and (um) rehabilitated. They'll be good as new in weeks if not days, of that you may be sure. Of that you may be sure!

Marta's third try at a match proved to be the winner. Satisfied with the smudge of color now drying to flat, pale blue on the pebbly, plastered wall, she set about mixing a larger batch in the best of her four roller pans. Done in a flash! She was good at her work, ten years in the trade, like it or not. Ready and steady with the roller, her favorite piece of equipment. Not slapdash like the cart, no. The roller even had cambered grips made of molded leather, sized precisely not just for any three fingers and thumb, but for her particular three fingers and thumb. A gift, five years back, from Avaun's father. "You cannot choose your work," he'd said, "but you can choose to do it well."

No need for the extension rod, this was ground-floor stuff. Dip and trundle, roll off the excess, and up to the wall. Drips allowed, you can't help it with paint, and the cobble will gobble, as D'Nan always said. After a hard rain or two, only the most egregious spills would show. But Marta never spilled, as D'Nan well knew. No gobbling cobble for her. The paving stones beneath the walls where she worked always retained their original color.

She was done before she knew it, and out came the househusbands to congratulate her on her quick response, her steady hand, her excellent coordination of color. Was she really the only paint-over artist in the whole city? Well, wasn't that something. Municipal Beautification! Terrific department, terrific. If we don't have the best Broman in the nation, I'd like to know who does.

But to all those many compliments—pack up, pack up, on to the next crime scene—Marta managed only half-intelligible murmurs. She didn't dare stick around—and why should she? "A seedling stared at never grows," her father's saying, had been inherited and adapted by Avaun to, "The noonday sun never sets." She'd once started to ask if he really believed that, but even framing the question seemed disingenuous, hostile, and she'd let it lie. He enjoyed saying it; perhaps that was all that mattered.

Off to her second wall of the morning, a temple of all things. Just how bold could this latest generation of vandals be? Bold as sharks, it seemed, for here was another statement entire, "Throw Down Our Walls!" Marta sighed and got to work. Walls. She worked on walls, she worked for walls. Throw them down? Never. As if anyone could. Coastlines were what her nation had, not walls. The sea was their bulwark against the rest of the world. Only at the isthmus was there an actual wall, somewhere high up on those legendary bare-rock peaks. Aesor's Teeth: even the name held people at bay. She'd seen the mountains, of course, but only at a great distance, and she'd certainly never seen the wall; too many travel restrictions for that. Easier to stay home, or at least not hanker for destinations too far east, too close to the rest of the mainland. Ten miles now, wasn't that the mandatory no-approach zone? And was it only one wall, or was it two? Avaun claimed he'd heard (from a friend of a friend of a friend) that now there were three. Which was baffling. Why did the *tathru* want to get in so badly? To steal ore from the mines? Mount raids for slaves? Invade for the sake of better cropland?

As she squinted at her first test mix of color––got it, first try!—she wondered if the walls on Aesor's Teeth were ever hit by vandals. Likely not. Slogans were meant to be read, and up in those heights, who'd be around to see?

It took until lunch to finish at the temple, and then she sat in the shade by a trickling, algae-smeared aqueduct and ate what Avaun had packed for her. The pear was especially good. Afterward, although she'd promised herself that she wouldn't, she headed back to Soldier's Square, leaving her cart behind. Unburdened, it was a quick walk, and she arrived in minutes, keeping her eyes downcast until she had a full view of the repainted wall, and then—damn.

The red lettering was already pushing through, the scarlet beneath turning her careful blue wall-work a dull, angry purple. She felt her fists clench. How was it doing that? What was going on?

A crowd had gathered, of course. A small crowd, but large enough. Pointing, whispering, wondering. Men and women both. They hadn't seen her, not yet—she'd taken precautions and entered the plaza at its far side—but they might at any moment. They'd be angry, thinking she'd done shoddy work. Except she hadn't. Unless––was it possible that D'Nan, whom she'd always thought a fair, compassionate supervisor, was setting her up to fail? Providing her with sub-par paint? No. That was ludicrous. Supplies didn't come from D'Nan, they came through Purchasing. A tidy, anonymous interaction. Surely Purchasing could have nothing against her; they likely didn't know her name.

A voice at her shoulder made her jump like a skittish cat. "Remarkable, isn't it?" said a conspiratorial tenor, the kind used to making friends easily. "It just refuses to go away."

Marta swung around, expecting—what? A drunkard? A vagrant? But no, here was a well-dressed youth hardly old enough to claim a beard. Handsome, though, in a careless, insouciant way. He leaned shoulder-wise against a barrel-loaded wagon, arms crossed, looking ever so easy with the world. He wore––and she noticed this, for it was odd in the heat––bulky black leather gloves.

He said, with the slightest of accents, "Your handiwork, isn't it? I don't mean the text."

Marta told him in no uncertain terms that it wasn't her fault, wondering all the while, where could he be from? The peninsula? The islands?

"No, not your fault at all," he said. "But even so. Trouble any way you slice it. Wait, look, this'll be fun. Here come the constables to clear away the gawkers."

It was her first time coming before the Broman, or at least her first time solo. She'd stood in this same audience hall when she came of age for work, but then she'd been presented as one of a group: all the young women born in her month and year from all across the city, and the townships beyond. Now it was just her, her and the Broman together in this dim, airless room, its windows shuttered to prevent tubespies from buzzing their way into the city's official business.

The Broman, vexed, paced around the hall's many support columns, and once she kicked out at a plinth with her huge, bare feet. "Unacceptable," said the left-hand head, hot-tempered and the most canine of the three. "Can you not handle a simple paint roller?"

On learning she'd been summoned, Avaun had counseled patience. "Don't be drawn into arguments. State facts. Express remorse if need be. Be willing, and dutiful. It's not your fault."

"It's not her fault," said the right-hand head, unknowingly echoing Avaun. This one had sleepy, heavy-lidded eyes, and spoke in a voice redolent of dusk and dreams and ivy.

"We suspect the interference of sorcerers," said the middle head, the so-called Justice Head, a stern, steady-eyed frowner. "Do you suspect the same?"

No matter Avaun's council, Marta hesitated. A dribble of sweat ran down her back, another down her sternum, down between her breasts, and of course the Broman could see it, for like all who were brought before the Broman, she'd been stripped naked. No, not stripped: too harsh, that, and unfair to the helpful attendants who'd steered her to a changing room. No one had touched her, no, but they had, with firm voices—so *parental*—given her to know that she must appear in the nude. Again, she'd heard Avaun: "You show yourself to me nearly every day, and with the Broman, it's tradition. Don't let that become the focus. Promise?"

The Broman's question hung in the stale air, awaiting Marta's answer. She said, her voice halting and stiff, "Of course, Beloved Servant. Sorcery. There can be no other explanation."

But the left-hand head had caught her hesitation as if it were a smell, a whiff of criminal musk. "No," she hissed, "she's got some other thought in that pretty head. Some sort of *scenario*."

"Oh, hush," said the right-hand head, now cocked to get a better look at Marta, Marta shifting this way, now that. How did one stand when naked and being interviewed by the Broman? What was the proper placement of the hands? Why wasn't this a known protocol, one taught in every school? Oh, but she knew the answer: you weren't supposed to *be* called before the Broman, not after your employment day. No, not even for a wedding, or childbirth. Bromans cared only for your work, your potential for diligence, your labors and your tasks.

The Justice Head spoke again. "You do accept the reality of magic?"

"Of course, Beloved Servant."

But she didn't. Could the Broman sense this? The left-hand head perhaps, with its glittering green eyes and too-obvious teeth. As a child, she'd believed, or thought she'd believed, but as an adult? No. True, she couldn't explain how seeds could make trees, or why the stars wheeled in the sky, but while these things surely were magic, yes, she had never seen spirits, or tree-goblins. No tables floated airborne, not in Marta's life, and did any house clean itself, without the help of a man? No. Never. And so, despite herself, despite a litany of mandatory, canonical beliefs, she suffered daily from heretical, crippling doubts.

The Broman shuffled her bulk across the floor, her heavy feet slapping and dragging at

the tile beneath. Outside the shutters, a tubespy arrived, probing to find a way in; the thrumming was unmistakable. Tubespies: now if those weren't proof of magic, what was? The damn things weren't alive, but the cunning of their manufacture! Unbelievable. They could *fly*. Sorcery for certain. As for the way they scrutinized every little thing, well! It was common knowledge, if not precisely official, that the tubespies could see and hear—and that the *tathru*, far away, could see and hear through them. Again, magic: pure, stinking magic. She'd told her children as much.

"Go back to your work," said the Justice Head. "From all reports, our city would be a wreck without you. Perhaps there is a different paint we may try. Some new mix. And We the Beloved Servant will inquire among the Council to see if they know of some trick, some amulet, perhaps, that will thwart this devilry."

"But ultimately," said the right-hand head, serene but with a lethal undertone, "it is you who will be held responsible. Do you understand?"

"Yes, Beloved Servant."

She crossed her arms at the wrists and let her fingers touch their opposite shoulders. This much protocol she knew; it was how one greeted or withdrew from any Broman, anywhere in the land. But if she'd had a knife right then, she might have tried to use it—yes, plunge it blade-deep to the back of the neck!—for she'd never been so angry. Needlessly so, of course. The Broman had every right to question, to investigate the situation. But anger fed on anger, as Avaun was fond of saying, and she all but fled for the changing room and the safety, however false, of her clothes.

Bedtime at home was a shambles. Nilo and Thuma weren't children at all, they were bright-eyed bundles of questions. What was the Broman like really? Did all Bromans look the same? Were you scared? Was she fierce? Did she hurt you? Help you? And I don't understand, why were you summoned? Are you in trouble?

She answered as best she could, and Avaun stayed close, his steady, settling presence a more effective balm than warm milk or the rush of evening wind through the pines. So many questions, so many half answers! Was she in trouble? Most assuredly. But not yet. Not exactly. And as for whether the Bromans all looked alike, she knew they all hailed from the same family, exceptional for its three-headedness, but beyond that, she couldn't say. She'd only ever met the one. She tried to use the moment to teach about bloodlines and traits, but the girls had no time for cogency, the considered answer. New questions leaped from their lips, swift as minnows. Do you go again tomorrow? Does this mean we get a bigger house?

Of course Avaun had questions, too, later, questions born of wisdom and worry, for he, too, knew fear. Long after Marta drifted into her usual solid, unmoving sleep, he lay staring at the ceiling, aware that despite his best wardings—doors, chimneys, every window— and despite his care in never letting the coals in the hearth die out, some new presence had entered their home, something perhaps not directly evil in its intent, but malignant nonetheless. It might not mean them harm, no, but did a storm at sea have any grievance against the unlucky sailors in its path? No. The wind was simply wind, and some days it blew hard.

Avaun slept at last, and the pines outside the window quivered, restless in the dark.

By the end of ten days, Marta no longer made any pretense of calm. Random vandalism she could cover over as before, but the huge red lettering, the slogans, they defied her. The Broman's alternate mix of paint was no better (and possibly worse), and complaints became

rampant. What was Marta up to? When was the city going to train a new paint-over artist, one

who knew her business? What would visiting travelers think? It was a disgrace, that's what it was. A scandal.

She wished she could catch whoever was marking the walls and wring her neck. Or his, perhaps. Curfew-breakers were the lowest of the low to start with, and as for folk who desecrated other people's property, there were no words—until now. She imagined herself coming up behind such a one, catching her in the act, spinning her round, shouting, grabbing hold, alternately strangling and punching. Blood and missing teeth, Marta on top, her fists a hail of righteous anger. The Broman would be pleased, the perpetrator hanged. Marta would receive a medal—and perhaps a work placement she would actually enjoy.

With or without enjoyment, in work she could still lose herself. As if sinking into deep water as it closed, gurgling, over her head, she could disappear into the process and effort of erasing each fresh slogan. But trudging home in the late afternoons, sunbeams slanting, jubilant gulls wheeling overhead, that was a nightmare. Giant red lettering, painted over only hours before, chased her home. "Ask The Dangerous Questions!" "Freedom!" "Worldwide Union!" Even with her eyes fixed on the ground, she could not escape.

Avaun chewed his knuckles, and he grew careless in dressing the children, prepping them for school. He blinked too often, as if specks of dirt pricked his pupils. When Marta came home, did he ask after her day? No need. He knew at a glance where things stood.

It was at an alleyway wall not far from Old Sesten's net-shop that the gloved man found her again. She'd nearly finished covering over the lettering ("Emigrate!") when he approached, his boots clicking on the paving stones like tiny scuffing hammers. He stood back, hands on hips, surveying her work. He took off his gloves, tucked them carefully into his belt, and let his hands splay again, oh-so-deliberately, on his hips. She was meant to notice. He had four fingers, five including the thumb. Five!

"You can't win," he said, as if that were a good thing.

She said nothing. Those hands, those ugly, awful fingers. He was a *tathru*. He had to be. Five fingers—she'd always thought that was rumor, fable-telling—but there he was, in the flesh.

The man sighed and raised one hand. He said, waggling his fingers, "You probably think it's magic. But it isn't."

"I don't believe in magic."

Eyebrows up from the five-fingered man. "Really? That's not the usual line."

She fixed him with a baleful stare, leaning hard on her roller, its head in the pan and shedding pale brown paint. "Are you," she said, and she was furious to find that her voice was quaking, no more steady than her wobble-wheeled cart, "are you the one who's doing this to me?"

"What if I were?"

That cheeky half-smile, she really would knock his teeth in. He was taller, perhaps heavier, but she'd have surprise on her side. Conviction, too. She leaned the roller against the wall and took a step forward.

The *tathru* man splayed his hands in front of him in a grotesque (too many fingers!) gesture

of peace. "I can tell you how it's done. Nothing to it, really. Bacteria. Specially trained to eat paint. Well, not *trained*. And you don't have a word for "bacteria," not exactly, but think of them as the really small things that live inside you—well, that live inside practically everything. So what I'm talking about is science. Applied science. We've embedded this red paint with bacteria that eat paint of almost any other color. For food, I mean. They digest paint. They're dormant when the paint's dry, but when you add a new coat—it's really very simple."

She'd taken another step forward. He'd taken three steps back. He said, hands still up to ward her off, "I can demonstrate, if you like. We'd have to do a little traveling, but I could show you."

"Leave us alone."

"Can't do that," he said. So apologetic, the five-fingered man. He sounded, even through the wall of her anger, genuinely sorry. "It's time you people joined the rest of the world."

The rest of the world? The *tathru*? Join them? For what? Why? Nothing he said made the least sense.

"This is what I *do*," she said, gesturing back at the wall, her cart, everything. She stooped to pick up a loose stone, fist-sized, perfect for hurling or crushing a grown man's skull. "You show your face one more time, and I'll kill you."

No smile now. The tightness of the alley, her sudden march toward him—he turned and fled. She clattered after, then leaned back to throw her stone. Running pell-mell, he flung back one final over-the-shoulder cry, "You people cannot hide out here forever! You can't!"

The rock sailed past his shoulder, nearly nicked his ear. Then he was gone.

A tubespy followed her home, whizzing around like a demented, overfed dragonfly. She tried to swat at it, but it kept its distance. She thought back to when they'd first appeared, perhaps a dozen years ago, and how she'd always imagined them as having tiny pilots inside, not just gears, sprockets, and screws.

Tiny pilots equipped, had such things really existed, with ten tiny fingers.

Avaun was not practiced at emergency thinking. Other than sitting watch over fevers with the girls when they'd been little, his had been a predictable, tranquil life, the kind that could be weighed through pipe-smoke and slippers. He knew himself to be industrious, but only within the confines of the homestead, of the roles to which he'd been born. Yet now some covert spark had been lit within him: a hot, burgeoning pressure, wing-like and expanding, all born of Marta's encounter with the *tathru*. Marta who lay snoring, curled in bed beside him.

Two facts rose uppermost in his mind. First, it had been ten days since her summoning, and she'd failed to erase a single slogan. No matter that she'd failed while using the Broman's own paint, she would be held responsible.

The second point was equally damning. Marta had come in direct contact with a living, breathing *tathru*, and she'd done so without the official imprimatur and strictures of a humanitarian rescue. That meant there were *tathru* living among them, which was bad enough, but it also meant—no. He couldn't face the outcome, not even for a moment. Or could he? His stolid mind was aflame now, and it tricked him—minds do that, yes!—and he imagined Marta tied to a stake in the main square, choking on pungent oak-log smoke as flames rose at her feet. The whole damn city would gather to watch. He and the girls, they'd be forced to stand at the front. Marta screaming, twisting against the ropes, would writhe in pain just yards away.

No. He wouldn't be the man who waited for the constables to come knocking. That would be madness.

He rose quietly and began his preparations. This was difficult, for at first he was of two minds: the mountains, or the sea? Both were dangerous, but he'd never been a fisherman, and the wind was up, the pines were whispering. The waves this night would be like walls. No, it would have to be overland. Aesor's Teeth. For that, they'd all be needing their boots. Boots and rucksacks. A lodestone. Luck.

Drowsing, slumbering, Marta dreamed of olden days and bedrock gods, the kind that never changed—or at least were not supposed to. Now they carried messages done in bold bright red, and those words refused her every effort to look away. She rolled over, restless. The slogans followed.

Around her, packing quickly, Avaun continued his preparations. Would she argue, when all was ready and he woke her? She might. If so, he hoped he wouldn't have to carry her for long.

Mark Rigney has had over fifty short pieces find print in a gentle arc covering the last two decades, with stories in venues like Lightspeed, Andromeda Spaceways, Cemetery Dance, Black Static, Black Gate, Realms of Fantasy, and more. An upcoming piece is headed for Tales from the Magician's Skull in early 2021. Plenty of theatrical credits, too, with plays produced across the U.S., including off-Broadway, along with Canada, Hong Kong, Nepal, and Australia.

An interview with Tiffani Angus

Author of Threading the Labyrinth

Interview by Mark Bilsborough

I first met Tiffani Angus way back when at a science fiction workshop, the annual week-long Milford critiquing and networking event held in the wilds of rugged North Wales. She was a loud, opinionated, confident, witty and charming American ball of energy with a hundred and one things to say before pausing for breath and all of them sharp and to the point. I liked her immediately. She'd just started with her PhD and teased us with a fragmentary tale of the wreckage of a ghostly WWII fighter plane appearing through time half buried in an English Tudor garden. I knew then it would make a great story one day, just as I knew we'd all be seeing and hearing a lot more from Tiffani Angus.

You may have seen her at conferences – she's been getting regular slots on panels for years. Or you may be lucky enough to be one of her students at Anglia Ruskin University, where she leads the MA Creative Writing course. Or perhaps you've read her debut novel, *Threading the Labyrinth*. If so, I'm sure you're sold already on the Tiffani Angus journey.

I caught up with Tiffani just before Christmas. She was in fine form and we talked extensively about her novel, the overlaps and synergies between her writing and her day job and the world in general. I asked her what *Threading the Labyrinth* was about. "The quick elevator pitch is that it's 400 years in one English manor house garden, set in five specific time periods."

It's an engaging, dynamic story that jumps around in time, a concept that Tiffani deals with adeptly. "When I originally had the idea for writing it, it was supposed to be about the house and about how in different time periods the different philosophical ideas of how people were supposed to live would be mirrored in the house. I realised that that wasn't going to work because houses don't change that quickly, but I realised gardens do: they get dug up and redone according to whatever the fashion is at the time."

And what about the title? "Threading a labyrinth means to walk a labyrinth's twists and turns to the centre and back out again. There's a labyrinth mentioned in the early part of the book, but it's torn out and you never really see it, because the idea is of threading all these times together and all these people together and that's how you twist and turn to the centre and come back out again." Labyrinths were a feature of many traditional estates. "In WWII, German spy planes flew over England, and they took photographs... that show a labyrinth from the Tudor era in the ground, but that had been gone for hundreds of years. Nobody knew it had been there, but it had left a ghost behind. You just needed to be aware of how to see it."

The sequences of the novel are framed by a 20th Century character – Toni, an American – who inherits the dilapidated house and gardens. She grounds the story and serves to highlight ideas of change and preservation. "While she's in England looking through papers and looking at the place, weird things start to happen."

Inside this frame are four other stories of the people that worked in the gardens, set throughout time from the 1620s, with weeding women, subversive photographers, a returning soldier, the story of a changeling, and a conscripted WWII agricultural labourer – a Land Girl – "because I love Land Girls 'cause they're awesome." Needless to say, "all sorts of weird things happen to them."

That Land Girls feature in this book in some way cements its Britishness, and unusually for an American writer Tiffani Angus has captured the style and tone of its setting with panache and perhaps more accuracy than a British writer might (I'd have called the boots the Land Girls wear wellies, for instance, and I'd have been wrong. They were called gumboots back then).

> "The walled garden is the centre of all the magic."

Their stories interlink across centuries. "It's about how this place holds on to all these people and the energy they put in to keep it together and how all the incarnations of the garden exist in layers on top of each other." There are shifts in time and ideas but "the land holds on to the stuff that came before... it ties in with the idea that we leave behind traces, and so if you're lucky enough to build a garden you've affected the future in some way."

All through the narrative people try to knock things down and change things, but the walled garden stays the same. In one of the early scenes, one of the house owners wants to get rid of all the gardens and turn everything into lawn, but he goes and the garden remains. Even Nazi planes can't destroy it. But when penniless Toni is tempted to sell to a housing developer, the garden faces yet another crisis.

"The walled garden is the centre of all the magic," Tiffani says. "One of the ideas about the garden is it wants a keeper – and that's why it

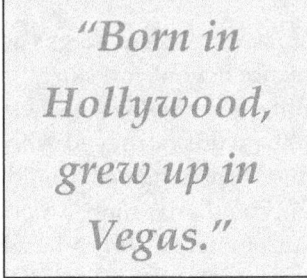

> "Born in Hollywood, grew up in Vegas."

does things like in the 1770s when it seduces the lady of the house. Toni showing up is like the eleventh hour for this garden – it's got to be saved so it does what it can to seduce her, too. The one thing it can give her is the idea of family and history. It's a bit creepy, but 'seducing' people is the only way the garden knows how to get them to pay attention to it."

I wondered how Tiffani's "born in Hollywood grew up in Vegas" background affected her writing, particularly as she's written a very British novel. The answer was a combination of having lived here for ten years and research – it must have worked because one of her early reviewers thought she was British and said she couldn't write in 'American'.

The contrast between the British and American voice is interesting, and one she was conscious of. "I had to rein in the American, but I insisted on American spellings in the American section because it felt weird to have an American with British spellings. I thought readers can handle that, and it brings home that she's not from here."

So why gardens and why Britain? "I decided to do a PhD. And decided I wanted to come to England because this is where the gardens live! I was a weird teenager; I would buy English gardening magazines because I grew up in the desert where there's no gardens and no green fluffiness, and so English gardens to me were always fantastical and strange.

"I spent years on the PhD doing literal field research where I would go to gardens all over the country and take hundreds and hundreds of photographs. I did lots of fun historical research on not just gardens but on everything from William Morris to food rationing during WWII to photographers – Julia Margaret Cameron in the Victorian era – to the drugs people would take in the Victorian era, to the names of plants in the 1620s – everything. And took it all and made a big pile of it and tried to figure out how it worked.

"I spent a lot of time going through each section and checking the etymology of words, to make sure the words existed. But there are things that cropped up that don't belong, like the hummingbirds. They don't exist here, but I put them in one spot on purpose. They show up in the 1700s when Thomas plants that seed from the Americas. A friend asked, 'Where did they come from?' and I'm like, he just planted a magic seed! It's literally a magic garden and you're asking where the hummingbirds came from?"

Gardens in fantasy fiction was a big driver of Tiffani's research, and it became clear that while "a lot of kid's fantasy books have gardens as central places, and most of them are some sort of time travel device," gardens feature less in adult fantasy or even adult fiction. "And even then the garden is often a place where murder and adultery and betrayal and all sorts of evil things happen." As she was writing, she realised she was creating "a grown-up version of these kid's books, such as *Tom's Midnight*

Garden or *The Children of Green Knowe*, and that hadn't been done before. I started to realise I was playing with time and with space in the garden and so (it) built out of there."

Threading the Labyrinth is in many ways unique but there are some common threads in *Outlander*– the series about someone time-slipping from the 1940s to the 18th Century Scottish Highlands. Gardens and the land feature prominently in both narratives and there are similar themes of custodianship and interconnectedness. It turned out that Tiffani was a fan. "I do adore *Outlander*, and any time travel stuff is inspirational but that one especially… When the first book came out… I got all of my friends addicted and they would call me and say, 'I was up until three o'clock in the morning and it's all your fault – I hate you.' There's so much more in the books than in the series. I mean it's sexy as hell and it's violent so, y'know, it's got all the stuff we love – sex and blood. And time travel and really good costumes.

"One of the very few fantastic garden books for adults is *The Moon and the Sun* by Vonda McIntyre. It's about Versailles during Louis XIV's reign, and his explorers bring back a mer-person and imprison it in one of the fountains in Versailles. I've always loved stories about Versailles and I've been there a few times. It's beautiful but it's built on the blood and backs of a lot of people who were not rich and so that's always been problematic, but it's this very strange place. Gardens are themselves so fantastical, such as 18th century English gardens being built to look wild. So you get these gardens that are supposed to look 'natural' but they've still got the hand of man on them – they're fake natural. And I love that about it – it's ridiculous!"

The gap between the war and Toni showing up isn't explored in this novel, which suggests there is room for more stories about the walled garden. "Possibly – I'm thinking about doing a short story collection with fantastic horticultural stories, because I've published several and I have the copyrights back, and so I think I'm going to do some *Threading* stories and then put it all together. In my head I've been doing a list of stories in different time periods, so I want to write about the nuns in the original abbey finding the changeling baby, and then something in the later 1600s with the emergence of the idea of science, then maybe post-war 1900s. We'll see."

> *I love that about it – it's ridiculous!*

She's got a novel on the go as well, started before the PhD that she's been trying to finish for years now, but "workloads and pandemics and everything keep happening. It's called *A Housewife's Guide to the Apocalypse*. This is about women in a post-apocalyptic America and how they deal with stuff – and then what happens to them because it's going to screw a lot of people over in very particular ways.

"I would love to finish a draft of *Housewives* in 2021 – that's my goal," she says. The research and planning have already been done: "Recently I went back to it to see where I was, so I got a big piece of paper and I drew/wrote what happened in each chapter that I'd written so far and started to realise where things need to be moved. I still have that piece of paper and it has arrows and scribbles and stuff all over it. I've got to a certain point, but now I've got to

figure what the structure is so I can go back and finish it correctly."

I wondered if Tiffani found it hard switching from short stories to novels. "I read the coolest analogy the other day. Think of a regular sized house, full of furniture like a two-bedroom house. And take that furniture and put it into a flat – it won't fit you have to edit it. That's a short story. And take that furniture and put it into a mansion, there's all sorts of space you going to have to fill, that's a novel. I could not write a short story until after I wrote a novel – it didn't make sense to my brain… a novel isn't just a long short story, it's a totally different thing."

Threading the Labyrinth has been well received so far. Tiffani has some thoughts about that. "A lot of people are doing comfort reading, so I wondered if in some way this was a sort of comfort reading, like something they liked when they were a kid. But perhaps there's also something deeper. There's also this idea in the book about your spirit living on in the history of the place, and the people that were in the place, and we're in the middle of a pandemic so this idea about holding on to the future and hope for the future I think is something that speaks to people. I think those all helped."

With an approach as creative and distinct as hers, it's little wonder Tiffani describes herself as: "an historical fantasy person who puts time travel in somewhere… The minute I insert magical flowers or something, people know it's fantasy. It's fun to mess with real people's lives – most of the stories I've written are based on real people who are long dead and the stuff they did – I've just messed with them."

Threading the Labyrinth is available now from Unsung Stories (www.unsungstories.co.uk) in bookshops and in all the usual places.

Souls of Smoke and Ash

Sydney Paige Guerrero

The first time Abbey ever saw a soul, she overate. She was in high school, dismissing her fatigue and inability to keep any food down as some kind of flu that was going around now that it was typhoon season, but she caught a whiff of something sickly sweet on her way to the classroom, and it somehow made her feel better and worse all at the same time.

She ran, her plain black shoes pounding against the white tiled floor of the school hallway, and found her classroom empty except for one figure shrouded in what looked like smoke. The smoke coiled around the figure, darker than the emissions from the exhaust pipes of the jeepneys that often passed by the small apartment she went home to, and the sight inexplicably made her mouth water.

If Abby had been thinking clearly, perhaps she might've realized that the figure was Sir Francis, her class adviser, but Abby wasn't thinking clearly. She wasn't thinking at all, too distracted by her instincts that were telling her that what she was seeing was a human soul, too focused on the way her vision narrowed, on the all-consuming hunger trying to crawl its way up her throat.

Abby doesn't remember much of what happened after she knocked him out, just remembers that the figure was gone and Sir Francis never showed up for class, which she was grateful for, because she got the distinct impression that he beat his wife so badly the night before that the woman ended up in a hospital. The floor was covered in a fine dust that clung to everybody's shoes for the rest of the day and Abby felt better than she had in weeks—in a bloated, *maybe-I-should-take-an-antacid* kind of way.

Abby doesn't know why she thinks of this now as she crouches over the unconscious man in front of her. Maybe it's because he looks like Sir Francis did, stocky build and too much hair gel, loud button-down shirt and thick eyebrows. In the dim alley lighting, she can almost pretend they're the same person.

Leaning in as close to the man's soul as she dares without actually touching it, Abby lets out a slight sigh. His soul smells sweet like overripe fruit on the verge of spoiling and it makes Abby slightly giddy, excited for her meal.

Maybe that's why she's thinking of Sir Francis. She hasn't eaten in a while and she might almost be as hungry as she was that first day. Maybe she just needs to remind herself of what happens when she gorges herself on someone's soul, of the restraint she needs so she doesn't lose herself in the miasma.

People are often wrong about what the soul looks like. Some seem to think that the soul looks exactly as the physical body did, down to every out of place hair and faded scar, as if the body was a mould that constantly changed the soul contained within it. Sometimes the soul is nothing more than a shape, the outline of a person held together so loosely that its edges constantly toe the line between substance and air, completely featureless and indistinguishable from another. Other times the soul is a light, small enough to fit in the palm of a hand, cradle against one's chest or release in the air like a paper lantern.

In reality, the soul isn't even inside of the body. The soul is a field of energy, thick like fog, radiating from the skin and dissipating outwards.

This man's soul is a murky gray haze that lets Abby know that he's not particularly good, but he's not particularly bad either. Her eyes turn into slits as she breathes in the heady smell. She unhinges her jaw and starts sucking in the man's soul, watching as the smoke-like substance funnels away from his body and into hers. It burns on its way down her throat, but

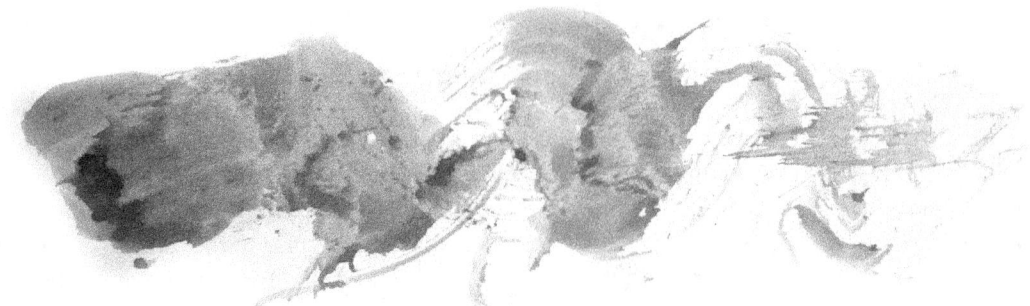

it's filling the gaping hole where her hunger festers. She craves more, more, *more*, but she wrenches herself away from the man. What's left of his soul returns to him, nothing more than faint little wisps rising from his skin like steam. It's not a lot, but it's enough, and Abby's learned that the human soul is like blood. Given enough time, it replenishes itself. Abby's passed by a few people that she's fed on in the past, their souls dancing around them as if she never touched them.

Wiping her mouth with the back of her hand, Abby struggles to get her breathing under control and presses herself against the alley wall. The soul swirls in her stomach. Now that the intake has stopped, it just stirs her hunger even more and she rides out the worst of her hunger's waves. By the time the soul finally settles, Abby feels a little less unstable, a little less desperate.

The man is still breathing, still very much solid and not reduced to dust, and for that Abby is relieved. Now that feeding isn't on the forefront of her mind, she sees the beginnings of a bruise are already forming under the man's left eye and Abby murmurs a quiet apology that he can't hear.

When she stands up, she spots his phone on the ground. He must have dropped it during the struggle. A generic picture of a sunset greets her, but she's distracted by the bold *4:51 AM* displayed on the screen.

Cursing, Abby tucks the phone into the man's hand and hurries out of the alley, hoping she won't be too late if she runs.

She's too late. Her father's awake and waiting for her in the living room of the apartment that they share, taking in Abby's disheveled appearance with a disapproving frown that she ignores as she makes her way to the kitchen. His soul swirls darkly around him like storm clouds before rain begins to pour. Abby has always wondered if his soul had ever been lighter at any point in his life and what caused it to darken. She's never seen it any other way.

"What you're doing is unnatural. It's evil. *You're* evil. Is this what you want?" her father says.

Who the fuck would want this? she thinks, though she's too tired to rehash this particular argument. Abby doesn't even know what *this* is. All she knows is that she is whatever her mother is—not that her mother ever bothered to explain before leaving Abby at six-years old. All she knows is that if she doesn't feed on her own terms, survival instinct will kick in and she'll feed on whoever's convenient until they turn to dust. All she knows is she is *not* a monster, no matter what her father says. She sees souls every day, after all. She knows what real monsters look like.

There was a time when she tried to make her father understand that, but at 18-years old, Abby's done trying to argue. She'll graduate from college soon anyway. She'll get a proper job and move out. Her father might want to keep playing the role of one-note telenovela *kontrabida*, but she's grown out of playing a helpless *bida*.

Instead of pleading with him, she meets his gaze and let her pupils turn into slits. He curses and makes a sign of the cross, but right now there's more fear in him than anger, and fear is something Abby knows how to deal with.

"*Demonyo*," her father says. "You belong in hell."

She smiles viciously, baring her needle-like teeth. "Maybe, but judging by the color of your soul, Pa, I'll be taking you with me."

She never does get to take a shower before leaving, which sucks because Manila has been criminally hot lately. Abby feels gross and weary before the day's even really started, so the blast of cool air that hits her face when she enters the café is a welcome relief.

Her coworkers are already here and Chris sends her to the bathroom the moment he sees her. "You look like a mess. Clean yourself up or else no one's going to buy anything. *I* wouldn't even buy coffee from you," he says.

"Good morning to you, too, sunshine," she says. She waves at her other coworker, Pia, as she heads to the bathroom in the corner of the shop.

She pulls her hair into a tight bun and splashes some water on her face. She tries not to look at her reflection in the mirror, but she sees it in her periphery anyway. It's always unnerving to look at herself in a mirror and see nothing but her own body. There's no haze around her, no energy that would indicate she has a soul, and sometimes she wonders if the reason she feeds on souls is that she doesn't have one of her own.

Her father's words echo in her head, but she shakes them off. Abby's already spent too many years dwelling in the usual teenage angst, compounded with regular existential crises about being half-human and half-*something*. In between having a shift to finish, a paper to work on during her break, and the usual amount of procrastination she usually does before buckling down to focus, Abby doesn't really

have time for anymore internal turmoil right now.

After leaving the bathroom, Abby helps Pia and Chris set up the shop. The shop's always busiest in the morning. They're not Starbucks or anything, but they're close enough to the universities that they always get a steady crowd of students and people on their way to work. After the initial rush dies down, Abby pulls out a few readings she needs to get done for her classes later, but ends up doodling in the margins when her brain starts to hurt from the abstract concepts in her philosophy readings.

She does a rough sketch of Chris, doodling his portly figure and using her pastel blue highlighter to capture what his soul looks like. His soul is bright, brighter than most people's souls these days, and most days the goodness inside of him outshines the bad. On those days, it's easier to see not just the blue, but the stoplight green and sunset orange of his soul too. Abby doesn't get nearly enough opportunities to figure out what all the colors mean since most people exist with the same cigarette smoke gray, but she doesn't have to understand something to admire its beauty.

Someone hums over Abby's shoulder and she turns to see Pia admiring the sketch.

"That's so pretty! Can I take a picture of it when you're done?" Pia exclaims as she watches Abby draw and Abby opens her mouth to answer when someone clears their throat.

The girl at the counter flashes them an apologetic smile and offers them a half-wave. "Excuse me? I'd like to order, please," she says, but Abby's not really listening, too busy staring at the girl to pay attention.

The girl herself doesn't particularly stand out as she waits in a plain white t-shirt and blue jeans, and it takes a moment for Abby to notice what's off about the girl. Then, she realizes with growing horror that not a single color emanates from the girl's skin, not even a shadow of a soul, almost as if the girl is soulless, but that's impossible.

Abby makes sure she remembers the face of every person she's ever fed on and she's sure she's never seen this girl before in her life. She doesn't even understand how this girl can be alive without a soul, to be moving and talking and ordering coffee instead of dust on the floor.

A sharp elbow to the ribs snaps Abby out of her reverie and Abby puts on her standard customer service smile before she can think too much about it. "What can I get you?" she asks.

"A mocha, medium, to go," the girl says.

"Alright. Name, please."

"Sara."

Abby works in a daze. She knows, of course, that she can't be the only one of her kind. Her mother was the same, so it stands to reason that there are others, but Abby didn't even know where to start looking as a kid. Now this girl is standing in front of Abby, waiting patiently as if she isn't potentially the answer to all of the questions Abby hasn't asked in a long time.

Logically, Abby knows that no good will come from meeting someone like her. Abby's been dealing with her condition, situation, whatever you want to call it, on her own for *years*. She's doing just fine working with her limited knowledge of everything. Abby might not be a monster, but she can't vouch for any other beings like her, and it's probably safer not to find out.

That doesn't mean she's not curious.

Abby tugs the ends of her hair in anxiety as Sara waits to get her coffee and only relaxes once Sara leaves with her to-go cup. Sara disappears into the crowded streets outside and when nobody comes into order anything, Abby goes back to her readings with renewed determination. Abby's had enough distractions for now and the last thing she needs is to focus on questions she shouldn't be trying to answer.

Sara returns to the coffee shop the next day, and Pia nudges Abby with her hip.

"It's the girl you were checking out yesterday."

Abby blushes and almost stutters out that *no*, that's not what she was doing, but realizes that she can't exactly tell Pia that she was staring because Sara is soulless, so she shrugs it off instead. "Whatever. You know I don't date," she says.

"What are you two whispering about?" Chris asks, carrying a tray of empty mugs.

"The girl Abby is totally not attracted to," Pia says and winks conspiratorially at Chris.

Chris rolls his eyes, but his lips are twitching as he attempts to hide his smile. "Gossip during your break and get back to work," he says, pushing past them before pausing to turn back. His voice drops to a whisper and he says, "Besides, Abby should probably get to the register so she can talk to the girl instead of wasting her time with your teasing, Pia."

"Traitor," Abby whispers back.

"Work!" Pia insists and pushes Abby to the register.

Sara orders the same thing, but requests so much sugar that Abby can't help but wrinkle her nose in distaste as she studies Sara from the corner of her eye. If Sara is like Abby, then maybe Sara can see that Abby's soulless too. Maybe Sara came back because she burns with the same questions, the stupid desire to know.

If Sara's doing anything like that, then she's doing an excellent job of hiding it.

Sara leaves with her coffee again, but comes back the next day and the next day and the next.

Abby likes to think that years of hiding what she is has afforded her some kind of ability to maintain her composure, but she finds herself growing more and more flustered every time Sara shows up, the need to ask *Are you like me?* struggling harder and harder to push past her lips.

It doesn't help that Abby hasn't eaten in a while, too swamped with requirements to find the time to get up early just to hunt for a meal. The hunger makes her frazzled and her weakens resolve. Still, Abby tells herself that she doesn't have much of a chance to ask Sara even if she wanted to since the girl always leaves the shop immediately after getting her coffee.

Then one day, Sara doesn't leave. She unexpectedly stays and takes the corner booth in the shop and Abby can't think of an excuse not to approach her.

Abby watches Sara for a moment and makes the rash decision to take her break already. It's only when Abby's standing next to Sara's booth that Abby realizes she has absolutely no idea how to start this conversation. *"Would you happen to eat souls on a regular basis? Yes? No? Oh my bad, that was totally a joke, so please don't complain to my boss because I really need this job,"* suddenly seems like a very unappealing option.

Luckily, Sara notices Abby hovering uncertainly and saves her from having to start the conversation. "Oh hey! Abby, right? You on your break? Class got cancelled and I could use the company," Sara says, like she's greeting a friend. "How's your day been?"

"It's alright. You?" Abby asks as she awkwardly take a seat across from Sara.

"Better now that class has been cancelled," Sara grins, and Abby returns the smile nervously.

"So, um, what do you study?" Abby asks. She hopes her attempt at small talk isn't really as strained as it sounds to her own ears, but she suspects it is.

"Economics," Sara replies. "I'm just glad that my hell week's finally over and I can relax a bit before the work picks up again. What about you?"

"Same. I mean, about hell week being over, not—not the economics thing. I hate math," Abby blurts out. "I study communications, which probably isn't obvious right now, but I swear I'm usually better at talking."

Without the haze of a soul, it's actually easier to see Sara's features than it is to see most people's, but Abby finds Sara much harder to read. Abby doesn't know how regular people get by without seeing souls. Facial expressions can lie, she knows, and she doesn't know if she

can trust the open and amused smile on Sara's face.

"You're doing fine," Sara says, then takes a sip of her coffee. Sara tilts her head at Abby as if considering something and nods to herself once she reaches a decision. "Hey, since your hell week's over too, what are you doing later? I feel like I've known you for weeks, but I don't, you know, *actually* know you, so if you're free, maybe we can hang out?"

This is a bad idea, Abby thinks, *this is a very, very bad idea*. Whether or not Sara's like her, Abby should probably turn her down. She knows that. But looking at Sara's soulless form and her own soulless hands, Abby wonders what it would feel like to have someone who understood.

"Yeah," Abby says. "Sounds great."

An afternoon turns to weekly meetups that turn to daily hangouts, and Abby gets to know Sara like she's never let herself get to know anyone else. Abby's never scared to look directly at her, to lean in too closely and accidentally lose control when she catches a whiff of a soul. Being with Sara is easy, so easy, and Abby can count on one hand the number of things that have come easy in her life. Abby knows she just has to be patient, to wait until she and Sara are close enough to ask Sara about her soullessness.

And if it turns out that Sara isn't like Abby, well, that's something Abby will worry about if it happens.

For now, Abby takes advantage of Sara's fondness of her and agrees to almost every proposed meet up, even choosing to spend her breaks in the coffee shop with Sara where they read in companionable silence. Abby spends a lot of their time together observing Sara, trying to find any hints of what she is. Sometimes Abby catches Sara watching her too and questions if Sara's looking for the same thing.

Some days like today, they hole themselves up in Sara's apartment. They use Sara's laptop to watch some American drama that Sara thinks is absolutely riveting and Abby thinks is absolutely ridiculous, drinking warm cola and sharing a too weak electric fan. It's on days like this that Abby forgets that she's supposed to be finding out if Sara eats souls like her, forgets about anything except the fact that she's having fun with a friend. On days like this, Abby is sure she's not a monster and she's pretty sure that no matter what Sara is, Sara isn't a monster either.

They both watch as some girl has an emotional conversation with a woman that Abby thinks is the girl's mother, and Sara groans dramatically at the scene.

"Man, I hate watching scenes like this. They make me homesick and now I want to call my mom. I'd regret it though, my mom never fails to point out that I'm not graduating on time," Sara says. "What about you? What's your mom like?" she says.

Abby shrugs. "She left when I was a kid," Abby says, picking at the peeling plastic covering of her Coke bottle before unravelling it in tiny strips that twist around her finger like string. She avoids looking at Sara and tries for what she hopes is a blasé tone. "It's whatever."

"No one knows where she went?"

"Maybe her parents, but I don't know them. All I've got is my dad."

"I kind of get it," Sara says, and Abby raises her eyebrows in surprise. "My dad died when I was young. All I've got is my mom," Sara explains.

"Oh," Abby says because she doesn't really know what to say to that. She's not sure if Sara's waiting for her to say something. Maybe Sara's dad ate souls and Sara grew up just as clueless as Abby did. Maybe Sara wants Abby to ask her about it, to confirm that they're the same, and this seems as good an opening as any.

"Hey, Sara?"

"Hmm?"

Abby considers asking, she really does, but something about the way Sara's looking at her makes her pause. Abby's never told anyone about her secret before and if Abby's wrong about Sara, then all of this will stop. No more

hangouts, no more conversations, no more friendship. Sara will think she's crazy and Abby will never see Sara again. Or worse, Sara will look at Abby the same way Abby's father looks at her. Abby doesn't know if she can handle another person's disgust.

Besides, they haven't reached that evolve or die stage yet, so Abby just shakes her head and swallows, her stomach stirring oddly, and she feels like she might be sick. "I just think we should watch something else," she says instead, and if Sara looks confused, Abby pretends she doesn't see it.

Over the next few weeks, things go smoothly: Abby feeds on a couple of muggers, no customers yell at her at the café, and Sara helps her out with her physics problem sets. Best of all, Abby's dad makes himself scarce. But, as good as it is to be away from him, it's also concerning. He might be going through another phase of *my-daughter-can't-be-a-monster-if-I-pretend-I-don't-have-a-daughter* or it could be like the time he set up a gallon's worth of holy water around the doorways of the apartment thinking he could wash the evil out of her.

The holy water thing didn't work, of course. It just drenched everything in her backpack and pissed her off, but she didn't burn.

Abby doesn't even want to think about the time he tried an exorcism.

The longer the peace in her life holds up, the more anxious she gets and the more anxious she gets, the harder it is to get some sleep when she's home.

Chris notices. She's become this weird mix of sluggish and jittery, nodding off when the crowd in the shop is slow and jumping at every little disruption. It's beginning to annoy Pia, but Chris chalks it up to her upcoming finals. He offers to let her take a few days off to study, but Abby knows those are days she won't get paid, so she declines. Sara notices too and gifts her tea that's supposed to be soothing.

Still, she starts to get worse, her entire body an amalgamation of aches, until she practically drags herself home when her shift at the coffee shop ends.

Maybe I just need to eat, she thinks, though there's still daylight and she'll have to wait until nightfall. When she gets home, her father's bedroom door is closed and she tries to finish some of the sketches in her notebook while she waits. The hours pass by slowly and by the time Abby deems it late enough to go out, she ties her shoelaces too tightly and starts to sneak out.

"I only ever wanted what's best for you," her father says.

Abby jumps, her pulse picking up as she turns to see her father standing in the living room like he's from some kind of shitty jump scare filled horror movie. She leans on the door and sighs in exasperation. "What the fuck, Pa? You scared me."

Her father ignores her and goes on talking. "I tried to protect you. Your whole life, I only tried to protect you," he rambles.

Ah, here it is, the calm is over and here's the fucking storm. Abby rubs her temples to ward off the headache she can feel building behind her skull. "Yeah, Pa. Great. Thanks for trying, I guess," she says and goes back to opening the door before he can pull out a wooden stake.

"I didn't get rid of her just so that you could turn into her," her father snaps and everything inside of Abby freezes.

Something like dread builds in her veins, creeps its icy hands all over her body and bangs its fists on her heart. She turns around to see her father has started to cry, the trails somehow glistening down his face from under all the smoke of his soul.

"What did you just say?" she asks.

"Everything I've done is for you. Everything I'm doing is for you. I'm sorry, I'm sorry," he cries and it's so different from the stoic, angry man that Abby is used to seeing that she can't quite process what's happening.

They're silent for a few moments, nothing but the sound of his quiet crying and her heavy breathing. When she reaches the inevitable conclusion, the realization isn't even earth shattering. The truth has always been there—in the way he talks about her mother, in the darkness of his soul. "You killed her."

"I didn't. I couldn't. I loved her, but she was a monster and I needed to save her from herself. She was going to hell. I needed to stop her," her father says, his words bleeding together as he stumbles through his sentences. "There was a man. I found a man who could help us, but she—she—but not before he—"

"How could you?" Abby asks, her voice sounding foreign to her own ears. She didn't realize that her eyes have turned to slits, that her body has taken on a stance as if she's about to lunge.

Her father takes a few breaths and steadies himself. He looks her in the eye with a pitying look that Abby hates more than anything else in this world. "I did what needed to be done. I thought I saved you, but she passed whatever she was onto you. I tried to find another way. For years I tried to help you, but now—now I have to save you too," he says.

It hurts in a way that her father has never hurt her before. He is never done teaching her fresh ways to ache. But she's not afraid. She's angry, so angry that for the first time in her life, she genuinely wants to hurt someone. She wants to tear away his soul and then tear apart what's left of him. She wants revenge for the mother she never really got to know. She wants to hurt him for all the years he tried to teach her to hate herself and for all the ways he's planning to 'save' her now.

He looks tiny now. Pathetic and nothing but a speck wrapped up in a toxic fog. Abby doesn't want any of that filth to touch her, but she'll spit it out after chewing his soul up if she has to.

"I love you, Abigail. I was too weak to do this for your mother, but I'll do this for you," he says, and then he lunges at her with a knife.

This isn't the first fight Abby's ever been in and she moves to dodge, but she's not as fast as she usually is and he lands a sizeable cut on her arm. She manages to tackle him to the floor and the knife clatters to the ground. He tries to kick her off and she has trouble pinning him down, so she cracks her jaw open and starts sucking in his soul.

Abby has never consumed someone's soul without knocking them out first, but she can't afford her father that courtesy. Eventually, he stops struggling and his limbs flail aimlessly, his mouth open in a silent scream. Abby recognizes the point just before she takes too much, feels the invisible ceiling she's trained herself to never move past, but this time she forcefully sucks in more of his soul, practically slurping its filth. His body begins to crumble, dissolving into ash and collapsing completely once she swallows the last of his soul.

By the time Abby pulls back, her father is gone. Her hands and knees are covered in his ash and a wave of nausea hits her hard. She starts retching on the floor, a black slimy substance spilling from her mouth. She feels dirty—*disgusting* because impressions of her father's thoughts are swirling in her mind and she doesn't want to understand him. She just wants him gone. She doesn't want any part of him, not even this human-half he supposedly gave her, but he's everywhere. He's scattered all over the apartment, on her clothes and in her hair and in her mind.

She curls up on her side, cradling her bleeding arm against her chest and starts to cry. The last time she ate someone until they turned to dust, their voice whispered in her mind for weeks until they finally went away. The beginnings of her father's voice is scratching at her brain and buries her head against her knees, wanting nothing more than to disappear.

What have you done, Abigail? Look at what you are. Demonyo, demonyo.

Abby almost misses the sound of the door opening. Her head snaps up just as Sara walks into the apartment.

"Fucking old man. Tried to change his mind and look where that got him. I told him to let me handle this. What a mess," she says, scowling at the dust on the floor.

Blinking, Abby pushes herself up and shakes her head to make sure she's not imagining things as Sara closes the door and takes a step closer.

I will save you, Abigail. You'll see.

"Okay, I guess I don't have time to draw this out anymore. I'm going to ask you questions and you're going to answer them," Sara says, pulling out a gun and leveling it at Abby's chest.

Abby doesn't recognize the blank, almost bored look on Sara's face and it frightens her more than the gun pointing at her. "I don't understand," Abby says.

Sara rolls her eyes and gestures at Abby. "You come from a family of monsters who eat souls. I come from a family of heroes who kill monsters. Your mom actually killed my dad, but he killed her too, so we're even. Don't worry, this isn't a revenge story or anything. Your dad hired me. It's nothing personal, really."

Abby can't even bring herself to feel betrayed, just hopelessly disappointed. She thinks of all those months Sara came into the coffee shop, all the days they hung out, all this time she has tried to be a friend to Sara. If not even Sara can see her as anything but a monster, then who will? "Why didn't you just kill me the moment my father told you about me?" Abby asks. "Why wait? Why now?"

"Because you're half-half and I've never encountered a halfy before. I wanted to study you first, figure out what I was dealing with because unlike most of my family, I ask questions first and shoot later. I wasn't going to kill you until I found out as much as I could, but your dad bumped up the timetable. Anyway, we're getting off topic. *I'm* supposed to be asking the questions, not you," Sara says, clicking the safety off her gun. "You know any other soul eaters? Pal around with any *aswang?* Late night trysts with *manananggal?*"

Abby presses her lips together and looks away. Her arm hurts and she's not in top shape right now, but she thinks she might be able to get the gun out of Sara's hands long enough to—to what? There's still no soul that Abby can see and unless Abby can subdue Sara in a purely physical fight, she's not sure how she can win this.

"See, now I know you're thinking of a way to fight me because you're terrible at keeping on a poker face," Sara says and continues talking in that same monotone voice. "Did you know the taste of cola and certain teas are strong enough to mask the flavor of a potion? Especially potions designed to weaken your kind?"

The expression on Sara's face isn't even smug. It's an exasperated kind of patience that pisses Abby off. Abby's eyes turn to slits as she bares her teeth at Sara. "Fuck you, you soulless bitch," she says.

"Oh, I've got a soul. It just takes the right type of magic to hide it, but I really don't think you know much about magic or anything about the supernatural world," Sara says. "Here's what I think: I think you don't know any soul eaters. I think you don't know the full extent of what you can do. I think I made a mistake of trying to extract information out of you like this. I think you might be more useful on a dissection table."

Aggression is getting her nowhere, so Abby decides to switch tactics. Abby relaxes her features so she looks more human and lets the hurt and fear she feels show on her face. "Why are you doing this, Sara?" Abby says.

"You're a monster who takes people's souls. I don't need any other reason," Sara says.

Abby's tired of people telling her she's a monster and she's tired of trying to convince people she's not. She thinks of Chris and Pia at the shop, of the classes she's almost finished and the diploma that was just within her grasp. She thinks of the half-finished drawings in her notebooks and all the things she wanted to do. It doesn't matter how she lived her life, she realizes, she was always going to end up here for living in the first place.

"I don't want to hurt anyone," Abby says anyway, already feeling the futility of her words. "You know that. You have to know that."

Sara shakes her head, the slightest shadow of a frown passing over her face. "What I know is that you're a monster," she says, pointing the gun from Abby's chest to her face.

Abby thinks of another conversation just like this, only she was the one at the door and her father was standing where she lies now. Abby smiles again, not as viciously as when she smiled at her father, but sadder. Resigned. "Maybe," she says, "but so are you."

Then, Sara shoots.

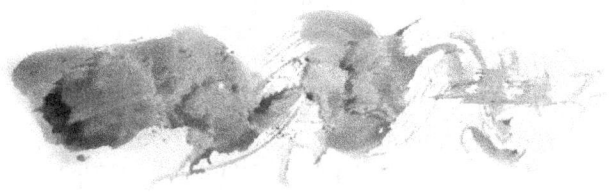

Sydney Paige Guerrero graduated from the University of the Philippines, Diliman with a degree in Creative Writing. Her fiction has won two Nick Joaquin Literary Awards and has been featured in Daily Science Fiction, The Philippines Graphic, and other venues. Her latest stories are forthcoming in Philippine Speculative Fiction 12 and Translunar Travelers Lounge. Currently, she teaches at the Department of English and Comparative Literature at the University of the Philippines, Diliman, and is the managing editor of an upcoming sourcebook for Philippine speculative fiction.

The Klizzys

Bonnie West

Your father swerves the truck hard off the highway. The bucket of fish you're holding steady between your legs sloshes lake water onto your shorts and the floor. He hops out without noticing and you follow fast without wiping it up or saying a word.

He points at the billboard on the edge of the road, high above you. "Look at that antenna thing on top. Never seen things sticking out of a billboard before." He pokes your skinny arm with what used to be his thumb. When he was a boy he blew his thumb off with his own shotgun and it seems to you he jabs you with that stump every chance he gets. He's told the story hundreds of times, maybe to teach you and your brother a lesson or maybe he just likes how the thumb flies farther, getting bloodier, with every telling. You sometimes lie in bed biting the skin around your ragged fingernails thinking about that thumb, wondering if animals ate it, nail and all.

Over the top of the billboard a metal rod stretches high into the darkening sky and ends with a golden, spinning ball. Green neon lights flash the call letters of the local radio station, K-L-Z-Y, one after the other, around the ball.

"The Klizzys," you say.

Your father looks down at you and you point back to the huge family pasted on the billboard. A woman sits in a rocking chair and knits. A man is smoking a pipe with a little brown dog perched on his knee. And two kids, an older boy and a girl around seven, who looks like you, lie on the floor listening to an old fashioned radio as if big news is coming. "It's their name in lights," you say.

He looks up again and says the letters out loud, "K-L-Z-Y," then adds, "Well, aren't them Klizzys a nice, normal looking family."

You imagine something bad happening to that nice, normal family. Something bad enough to rock the woman out of the chair, her yellow ball of yarn flying, start the dog barking and the kids screaming. You imagine the whole scene melting like a photograph burns when you light a match beneath it. Goodbye nice family.

"Wish I'd have invented something like that billboard antenna. Some guy got a bucketful of money thinking that up." He sets his hand on top of your head and swivels you back towards the truck, flicking his cigarette onto the street. While you're climbing in he reaches behind the seat and grabs a beer. "Jesus, what'd you do? Dump those fish?"

He revs the engine and peels out. You flip around to look through the back window, to watch gravel spinning out, and watch the Klizzys and their little dog shrinking smaller and smaller as you drive away.

Your mother, Donna, holds the screen door open with one hand, flaps the air with the other, "There you are. Hurry up and don't let mosquitos in."

Your father drops the bucket in the mudroom, lifts and swings the stringer of walleye onto the knife-worn wooden counter, then goes to the fridge for another beer.

"I wish you wouldn't, Dell," she says.

"And why shouldn't I? Like I can't tell you've been in the bottle the whole goddamn day? And what the hell is this?" He points to a blackened loaf of macaroni and cheese she's pulling from the oven.

"You don't always catch 'em," she says, turning away from the oven to look at him. She burns her hand on the loaf pan and swears at the burn or at him.

He pulls a filet knife from the drawer and pretends to jab her with it, like a joke but not a joke, then guts the first fish.

You leave the room.

You can hear them arguing back and forth, your mother telling him he's so mean and your father's answer nothing good enough for her royal highness.

 You go into your room. You spend most of your time alone, so you are surprised when you hear a voice, a whispery, high voice, saying, "I hope they won't step on us." You turn to the sound coming from the dollhouse your dad made for you, the dollhouse with its balconies, swinging doors, and tiny shingles, the dollhouse you still play with. You haven't yet taken the boy away from the family of four sitting around the table. But you think you should, even though it will make you sad.

You kneel down to peer inside and instead of the wooden family sitting, immobile since you last fiddled with them at the dining room table, you see four living people standing together on the porch looking back at you. You know them instantly, the family from the billboard. The Klizzys. When you wonder to yourself if the dog needs a water-bowl, he barks in response so you reach high on your bookshelf in search of the small sewing kit you got from Santa but never used because that year you'd asked for a heavy- duty rod for muskies. You unzip the plastic lid and take out the silver thimble, go to the bathroom, fill it with water and without spilling a drop, set it in the dollhouse on the kitchen floor. The dog drinks and wags his tail.

When you beckon them by thinking, come out of the dollhouse into our living room, they do.

You never have friends come over any more. You didn't have that many friends to begin with, and now you've ignored the few you had. You hated all the neighbors showing up, one after the other, rows of sad faces, hands bearing hot dishes wrapped in kitchen towels. You hid behind the couch where the Klizzy dog is sniffing now, probably for mice that skitter along the quarter-round molding at night. You think the dog might stick his nose in a peanut butter trap but he doesn't. He's smart, like the mice. The dog jumps up on the couch and turns himself around and around before settling down exactly Wally always sat when you watched TV and ate Fritos. Now the smell of corn chips makes you sick.

You remember how your mother used to say there were ten years between you and Wally because you were a mistake. She only added happy mistake if someone was in earshot. She no longer says it.

Sitting in the living room, you listen to the Klizzys talking to each other. The children tell each other jokes and Mrs Klizzy relates jolly stories. Mr Klizzy says things are swell. They talk like the family on your favorite television show, Leave it to Beaver. You love it that Wally's name is Wally like the character in the show and you think of yourself as the Beave the little brother, even though you're a girl. The only voices you hear with your ears are those of your parents arguing in the kitchen. Too polite to comment, Mr Klizzy tamps his pipe and Mrs. Klizzy rearranges her knitting, continuing to work on a very complicated sweater-vest, using a third, shorter needle, which clicks along with the other two.

Wally was killed in a hunting accident. At least that's what your folks say when they don't want to explain the whole thing. But when he died, he and the other guys weren't shooting guns. They were just goofing around. After waiting hours for the pheasants to fly, they gave up. They jumped back in the car, and Wally, instead of getting in, hopped on the hood just as it began moving. He flipped off and just like that, got run over. They dragged Wally into the back seat and raced to the hospital, but by the time they got there he was dead.

Now you're on your own most of the time. Your parents are here but absent. Wally is gone, but everywhere. Nothing is the same.

Your mother spends hours in Wally's room where she says no one can go. You went in first chance you got and lay on the bed spinning and spinning his blaze orange cap on your fingers. You put your tongue on bloodstains still on the brim. Your mother charged in and grabbed it from you, yelling for you to get out.

You wanted something of his for your own so the next time you went in his room you searched until you found his watch in the bedside table drawer and you hid it far back in your closet, in one of the patent leather shoes you wore to his funeral. You swapped your pillow for his.

Your father spends most his time in the basement but hasn't accomplished anything as far you can see. You wonder what he does down there now, since you never hear the sound of saws or hammers or B Bop music. Before Wally died, your father would come up from the basement whistling, sawdust on his clothes, and paint on his hands. In the basement, he made that whole dollhouse as a surprise for your fourth birthday.

Now you are a little afraid of both your parents and you think they should be a little afraid of you. You don't know why you have this thought.

"Dinner's on." Your mother leans through the swinging door gesturing into the kitchen. You don't invite the Klizzys to eat with you since dinner is never a good time. Fights heat up at dinner. Even before Wally died, family time wasn't fun. Even at Christmas, when people were supposed to be joyous and decking the halls, the tree meant fights about lights, ornaments, and tinsel. It had been Wally's idea to start decorating the tree in the morning. He said it would be better in the daytime because when night came and the tree was lit up it would be like getting a whole new tree to celebrate. He didn't have to say no one drinks in the morning. And he was right; it was way better. Wally had some great ideas.

The month after Wally died, there was no Christmas tree. No one wanted one. Well, you still did, but knew better than to say. Plus now they were drinking in the morning.

Your father has a couple more beers with dinner, and he starts getting a look that makes your stomach pitch, but out of nowhere it's gone and he's talking about the billboard, the antenna, and the lights, saying how clever you were making up a name for the billboard family.

You jump in then, "The Klizzys! They came home with us."

"What?" Your mother turns to you, "You brought someone home?"

She looks like she does when people come uninvited to the door, and she has to rush around straightening magazines, tossing laundry from the piles on the couch into bedrooms, slamming doors and drawers, and popping mints into her mouth.

"The kid's a hoot, Donna. K-L-Z-Y you know, the radio call letters. She named the billboard people Klizzys."

"Not on the board anymore," you say cleverly, thinking your father's word to yourself.

Your mother gets up and leans through the kitchen door to look in the living room. "Very funny," she says, coming back to the table.

"What, you thought they were real? God, you are a dunce." Your father rolls his eyes at you like you're sharing a joke.

"But they are real," you insist.

Both your parents say, "Enough," at the very same moment. They could say Cokes! You owe me a 10¢ Coke, like you and Wally use to say, but they don't.

As quickly as the good conversation got going, it dissolves into the bad one. Your father tells your mother she over-cooked the fish. She cries and says between gulps of wine, "The evening's a shambles." Glup. "It isn't funny to joke about people in the house." Glup. And finally, "You couldn't be happy that he fished with you all the time. He had to hunt too."

"Of course he wanted to hunt. Everyone hunts," your father yells.

"And now he's dead," she says.

You hope the Klizzys aren't hearing any of it and stream the words monkeysinabarrel monkeysinabarrel monkeysinabarrel through your mind to confuse them, but then see how your father is starting to cry too and you reach over and set your hand on his forearm.

He looks at your hand. He doesn't look up but whispers so softly you have to lean in, and maybe you think you hear him say, "Why wasn't it you, instead?" Then he stands, pushes his plate to the middle of the table, and lurches out the back door.

You leave your mother sitting alone after she doesn't say anything to make you feel better, even though nothing can make you feel better.

You're still awake hours later, when your father opens your door. The dog growls, from the dollhouse porch, but your father doesn't care. He smells sour when he leans over you then sits down on your bed. You pretend to be asleep. He says he's sorry, then starts in again on how much he misses Wally. You think about how you miss Wally more than he does, but you never say to him he should have died instead. After a few minutes, he gets up, trips catching his foot in the ruffled bed-skirt, swears under his breath, and leaves.

You get out of bed and notice the tiny lights have come on inside the dollhouse and the Klizzys have come out on the balcony from the upstairs bedrooms. They ask if you're all right and if there's anything you need. You don't know what to tell them. They know you're not all right.

The next morning your mom leans through your door saying, "Breakfast, Honeybunch." She's acting like nothing happened, like she always does when there's a fight at the dinner table. Pancakes are usually reserved for Sundays but she's made them anyway and once you sit, she slides two from the pan to your plate.

Your father comes to the table and starts to sit, but you say, "Don't. The Klizzys are sitting there."

You expect him to snap at you, or ignore you, but instead he says, "Someone's been sitting in my chair," in the Papa Bear voice he used reading Goldilocks to you when you were little. He shifts over into Wally's chair despite the look on your mother's face. After he's eaten, he says, "Maybe I should set my plate on the floor so the dog can lap the syrup." You like the idea, but you don't say anything. You aren't ready to forgive him. Your father sets his plate on the floor anyway.

"I'll be late tonight," he says before he leaves the house. "There's a big bunch coming in from New York City." He says New York City emphasizing each word. "Let's hope they're big tippers."

Your father works as a fishing guide for two of the fancy resorts on Bay Lake, taking groups of men who arrive, often from as far away as Texas and even once Japan, on a Minnesota wilderness experience. Men like him. He is, your mother says, "A man's man."

"All it takes is one to get the ball rolling," your mother says as he leaves.

Once your father had you come up to him in front of some departing guests and hand him an envelope. As instructed, you said, "My dad almost forgot to give you this."

"What's this?" your father asked, as if you were a stranger.

"A big tip!" you answered, running off across the parking lot.

You and your family don't live on Bay Lake but live nearby on Tame Fish Lake, where he never brings clients. "Gotta keep the best spots for us," he said to Wally, who helped out the last couple summers before the accident. Wally was going to finish his senior year, then he and your father were to going start their own fishing guide business. They were even thinking of adding hunting trips in the fall. In preparation for their enterprise, the first thing your father did was to carve a ferocious looking walleye and display it on a big sign between the wood-burned words, We find 'em. You fish 'em! Dell and Wally Swenson. There was also a delicate wooden holder at the bottom for the business cards Wally was going to design.

The last time you went in the basement the sign had been taken off the wall. You ran your fingers across the blackened letters thinking one day, when you got bigger, your father might make another one with your name. You could be a fishing guide, easy.

You love the basement with all your father's tools and carvings. You think about two months from now, when you'll have to go back to school. You won't bring the Klizzys with you. You don't even entertain the idea. It was bad enough having a dead brother, the way they looked at you.

You hope the Klizzys might spend their time in the basement with your father, who, during the winter months, used to build and paint birdhouses and whittle flat-plane Swedish figures with pointed or floppy hats, axes and beer mugs, long chins and funny noses, to sell at the resort gift shops every summer. You imagine the Klizzys might help name them, Anna-Lisa, Bosse, Kalle or Ebba, like you did whenever he finished a new one. He didn't carve any during the winter after Wally died and worried how much money they'd lost. Your mother told him it didn't matter about money, and sobbing, added, "I still buy too much food. He ate so much."

You know your father won't let the Klizzys down there with him even if he starts again. You know this because after a few weeks it's clear your parents don't like them. Even though you remind them not to shut the Klizzys in a closet or slam a door on them, your mother occasionally does just that. Your father says he's no longer impressed with your clever imagination. One night he asks if you really need so goddamn many of them, a father, mother, sister, brother and a dog?

It seems the less your parents like them the worse they behave. You've always tried to be good, to make every one happier, but the Klizzys, even sensible, quietly knit-one purl-one Mrs. Klizzy doesn't seem to care what your parents think. You see her raise her needles menacingly behind your father's back. The kids tear around the house even though you wish they would to hunt for pieces in the giant jigsaw puzzle at the card table or sit by the water and dangle their feet, but they don't sit still long enough. Instead they cannonball, screaming off the end of the dock, over and over, then run through the house scattering sand.

One afternoon your mother grabs you by the collar and spins you around. "How could you?" she screams. You know, and you also don't know, what she is talking about. She says things are being moved around in Wally's room. You say you will talk to them, you promise they won't do it anymore. You cry when your mother pulls Wally's watch out of her pocket and shakes it in your face. "They did not take and hide this in your shoe. You did."

Your mother won't let you take the Klizzies with you when you go with her shopping or to the library. You hate to leave them alone. You don't know what they might do.

One night you feel like you wake up in your bed, but you're not in your bed you're in Wally's room and the Klizzys are pulling his posters from the walls and tearing them into little little bits and dumping them on the bed and you're ripping all the photos from Wally's album photos of Wally holding Small Mouth Bass and Walleyes on the hook of his thumb, and photos of him standing proudly by the biggest Muskie ever caught in Bay Lake. Wally is grinning in all of them, and you see his grins dissolving as the Klizzys light the matches, and the paper starts burning, and the photos start melting, and the dog starts barking, and your parents run into the room and grab you and pull you from the fire, and your father throws buckets and bucket and buckets of water on the bed and floor until the fire is out and everything is wet. And then your mother and father pull you in their arms and you, all three, hold each other on the floor of Wally's room and cry and cry and cry.

The Klizzys are gone. You don't know where they've gone or if they'll be back. Even though they were chicken and ditched you, you miss them. But they also scare you. So when you think about it hard enough, you hope they don't come back. Every night you check the dollhouse, but it's always the same four figures who were there before the Klizzys came and now will stay since you've decided you won't take the boy away.

You wake up one night and swear you hear a dog barking across the lake. You wake your parents to tell them the dog got lost when the Klizzys left. Your mom brings you back to your room and strokes your hair as she talks.

"You know, I had an imaginary friend once. I hadn't thought about her in years although I did as soon as you brought the Klizzys home. She was different from them, she was alone, but I have to say it didn't end much better."

"Why? Did she do horrid things?"

"No, not really. I think my mother did the wrong thing though. A bit like me, I'm afraid." You don't understand, but she continues anyway. "My friend was a girl called Maryjane. Not so clever a name as your friends." You smile when she says that. "She was older than me and smarter and she was always hungry. I played with her, it must have been months, and we had great fun. But it always came back to her wanting to eat. I always asked my mother to feed her a sandwich when she made me my lunch, but she never would. She told me Maryjane could stay, but she wasn't about to waste perfectly good food on someone who wasn't real. I kept saying she was real, but it made no difference. Maryjane was stubborn too, so she wouldn't eat my food when I tried to share. She just got thinner and thinner and thinner. I got thinner too since I was only eating half my food everyday and my mother wasn't about to give me more. Then one day Maryjane got up from the table and said if she were my friend any longer she'd die. And with that, she was gone. I cried for weeks."

"That's a terrible story," you say.

"It is. And to this day, I don't understand either my mother, or me, for that matter, when it comes to Maryjane. But I do know somehow I got over it, and I was okay."

She leaves your room once she thinks you're asleep, and you hear her go into the kitchen, and you know she's pouring herself a glass of wine and you know somehow you can't have everything. But you also know you have something.

What you don't know is that when you are ten years old, your parents will take you to the pound to finally get you the dog that at least three times a year, you swear you've heard barking from the other side of the lake. They will do this to shut you up and will pretend it's nothing when you see a little brown dog, cowering in the corner of a kennel, who comes right over to you and licks your hand. You name him Izzy, even though your parents will suggest at least twenty other names.

And what you don't know is that when you are eighteen your father will establish his own guide business with his daughter (you) and Dell and Daughter Minnesota Guides will become known throughout the Upper Midwest.

And what you don't know is that when you are twenty-six your mother will sober up, then the next year, just when everything seems better, she will quietly divorce your father. Shortly after that you'll marry a man who, sometimes, in quirky ways, reminds you of Wally.

And what you don't know is when you are thirty you will have a child. And when she turns five she will have two imaginary friends who will frighten you but whom you will try very hard, to welcome with open arms.

Bonnie West has previously published essays and stories in Redbook Magazine, The Austin Chronicle, The New England Review and has a collection of short stories published with InkTears a small UK press. "Boyfriends" is available on Amazon. She lives and works in St. Paul, Minnesota.

Book Reviews

Mark Bilsborough

The Doors of Eden
Adrian Tchaikovsky

This is a new standalone novel from Adrian Tchaikovsky, the author of the highly acclaimed *Children of Time* and its follow up *Children of Ruin* (winner of the 2020 BSFA award). Both those novels deal with the evolution of sentient life in non-human forms, and this theme permeates *The Doorway to Eden* too.

The story begins on present-day Earth. Strange rifts are appearing and things from other versions of Earth are creeping through – neanderthals, giant rodents and worse. A student, Mel, falls through a stone circle in Bodmin Moor into a world of intelligent feathery dinosaurs leaving her friend, Lee, behind to try to make sense of her sudden disappearance. Then, years later, she's back with a new neanderthal sidekick and a heap of mysteries. It seems the multiverse is in trouble – and it's going to take a lot of brains from a lot of dimensions to make things right, even if that's a possibility. MI5 is involved – Julian and Alison – trying to locate then protect idiosyncratic scientist Kay Amal Khan, who has been whisked off to rodent world to work with Dr Rat (played with a straight face) following strongarm persuasion from the book's antagonist Rove, who's not that keen on preserving all the timelines, but has dreams that there'll always be an England, with the wilderness starting just beyond Berwick on Tweed.

I like this book. Tchaikovsky writes well, (if a little impenetrably in places) and many of his characters are nicely irreverent. There are too many of them in this book though, at least as point of view leads, and despite some broad brush signalling it's often hard to differentiate, say, Julian and Lucas, or Lee and Alison, all of who are given head space for their similar, overlapping thoughts. And Khan, personality wise, is photocopied straight from the *Expanse* series' Chrisjen Avasarala, the uber-cool take-no-prisoners Secretary General who never lets the opportunity for a good swear-fest pass her by.

The story sags in the middle and it's easy to get lost in complexity. But then it gets really strange towards the end with a sequence of short chapters that do something original that grab your attention and lead, satisfyingly, to an unexpected denouement (though as the book points out for much of its 597 page length, everything is possible, from ice-planet supercomputers to world covering sentient grass fields). Worth the soggy middle to get to the stimulating ending.

Goldilocks
Laura Lam

On paper this book sounded quite promising. Five women steal a spaceship and head off to a new planet, leaving behind a dying Earth. It's got some topical ingredients too – a global pandemic, a climate catastrophe, an ultra right wing misogynist US Government – and some intriguing character dynamics: a maverick scientist and her astronaut step-daughter, boyfriend inconveniently back on Earth in the ultimate long distance relationship, ex-husband in stasis on the ship as backup crew. Plus it's an easy read. And yet…

Plot first: set in the near future, Earth's climate catastrophe is gathering pace and the planet is rapidly becoming inhospitable; optimistic estimates suggest 30 years at most before total collapse. But there's hope: a new planet ten light years out called Cavendish, accessible though newly invented 'warp' technology. A mission is planned, a five man experimental starship called Atalanta, assembled in orbit. Men only, because US society at this point has become increasingly male dominated and women have been shunted to subservient supportive roles. Not quite *Handmaids Tale* (despite what the dust jacket might suggest) but enough to create a sense of injustice. So five women, headed up by the indomitable Valerie Black steal the Atalanta before the real crew can get there and head off to Mars, the staging point to Cavendish.

On the way to Mars things start to fall apart. People back on Earth are angry and here is talk of another spaceship to follow the Atalanta and bring the women to justice. The food supply on the ship gets compromised. The power starts draining. And Valerie Black becomes increasingly isolated and demanding. Crew tensions rise as they begin to make surprising discoveries about their mission – and their cargo.

It's implied in the prologue that the crew never makes it to Cavendish, which takes some of the heat out of the plot. Plus the narrative is peppered with a series of chronologically disconnected flashbacks which makes it all feel like a tale told rather than an adventure experienced. And some plotlines I'd really like to have seen developed (like why US society sidelined women and why the five felt they had to steal a spaceship) are glossed over whereas others (like the narrative lead, Naomi, having an unexpected pregnancy in space) are given prominence. And don't get me started on the frozen ex-husband wasted plot line – so much unexplored potential. Valerie Black, the antagonist, is writ large with no redeeming qualities and a ruthless zealotry. I like her, but it's hard to see what drives her, or why people should (initially) follow her so blindly or why a clearly capable and accomplished woman like her should so misread human dynamics in the way she ultimately does.

The logic for abandoning the mission and returning to Earth isn't entirely apparent, but is wrapped around the pandemic raging on Earth. Had I read this book a year ago I might not have noticed that the science behind the way this pandemic is described is, well, questionable. We're all pandemic experts now of course, so we all know about death rates of everything from ebola to flu, transmission vectors and the inevitable delays in getting a vaccine out into the general population. So there may be a case for a post-Covid re-edit here.

For me, the biggest disappointment is that this novel teases a new world (Cavendish) and the whole book is structured around the Atalanta getting there, only for the crew to decide to turn back at the last minute. It's like Christmas is cancelled at ten to midnight on Christmas Eve. The crew don't even seem disappointed, which makes you wonder why they wanted to go on the mission in the first place (not that was ever clear). That said, it wasn't hard to keep the pages turning in this book and just because I found some of the narrative choices unsatisfying others might take a different view. *Goldilocks* didn't work for me, but don't let that put you off.

The Poison Song
Jen Williams

This is the third volume in British fantasy writer Jen William's *Winnowing Flame* trilogy and it picks up right where the last volume, *The Bitter Twins* leaves off. The action takes place on the planet Sarn, where humans and Eborian coexist and face a common enemy – the Jure'lia, invaders who periodically devastate their communities. Now the Jure'lia are back. Previous novels detail the devastation and the fightback – but although the aliens may have been defeated, they are not gone forever. They are licking their wounds and returning to finish Sarn off for good.

There are fantastic characters in this series – apart from the dragons and behemoths and 'world devouring monsters' the Jure'lia, that is – like the archaeologist-adventurer Vintage, moody-Goth Tor and the frankly scary witch Noon – and that this novel can be so solidly character-grounded yet relentlessly action-packed is a testament to the quality of the writing on display here. Things unravel in this book – actions and events of previous volumes come back to haunt the protagonists. And the antagonists – the Jure'lia – are genuinely icky. Evil insects: what's not to hate?

I've been reluctant to give away too much plot information here because that would inevitably lead to spoilers for the first two books in the series – and believe me, you need to read them first otherwise you'll be completely clueless about the plot and not invested in the characters – so start with them and come back here if you need any more encouragement to read *The*

Poison Song. The first two, *The Ninth Rain* and *The Bitter Twins*, both won the British Fantasy Award in their respective years and I wouldn't take bets against *The Poison Song* completing the trilogy. Available everywhere. Go buy them.

World Engines: Destroyer
Stephen Baxter

I've read quite few Stephen Baxter books over the years and I've usually enjoyed them, though I've always felt there was something missing. He sets up ingenious plot situations and then lets the plot roll to see what happens. Problem is, I'm never too sure things would work out the way he assumes – for instance in his novel *Flood* sea waters rise and rise until the whole Earth is covered in water (not sure why– there's a hand-wavey explanation but no real logic) and people have a century or so to work out what to do next. But instead of a massive effort to build space colonies, underwater habitats, water-proof city-domes or (my favourite) country-size rafts of some genetically engineered sturdy floating sea-wood, there's one medium sized ocean going liner, a small underwater habitat and an underfunded colony ship programme. And nearly everyone dies. So, great setup, head-scratching thereafter.

Flood and its consequentials have been bugging me for years, to the point that I look at any new Baxter book with some trepidation. Will his instincts be so far away from mine to leave me head scratchingly frustrated again?

Well, yes. Plot first: Reid Malefant, (who also appeared in Baxter's Manifold series) wakes up five hundred years in the future (Buck Rogers? Not quite) where the world has changed and become much duller. AIs rule, the human population has declined sharply and no- one has to work anymore. This leads to inevitable listlessness, not least in Malefant himself, who was woken in response to a mystery signal from Phobos, purportedly coming from his dead ex-wife. Malefant gets very grumpy about everything in the future, apart from his new friend, inquisitive teenager Deirdra. Together they bully their way into space to see what's going on in Phobos, which turns out to be a massive artefact which acts as a pan-dimensional gateway.

Looming large in this version of Earth's future is The Destroyer – a massive new planet of extra-solar origin on a collision course with Neptune in… 900 years. Everyone seems resigned to their fate and the human race is engaged in a long wait to die. But not Malefant – which is why the planetary AIs send him out to Phobos hopefully to save the day.

The message from Malefant's dead wife turns out to be from a version of her – Emma – from another dimension. They come across a Russian from elsewhere too, and a shipload of Brits with comedy accents. Everyone is from a different what-if universe where Britain still has an Empire, or Neal Armstrong died on the moon, or Watergate never happened (etc), which is always fun to speculate with.

Then the plot shifts direction. Malefant is no longer grumpy (presumably because he now has something to do) and the Brits take everyone to the fabled ninth planet, here named Persephone, which is home to some strange alien 'towers'. I'd have stopped there to avoid spoilers but the book's title is 'World Engines' so I'm sure you can guess what the towers might do. Suffice to say, big things happen and a sequel is quite neatly cued up.

Does the story work? It's bitty, and has two distinct tones. When Malefant wakes, he's an angry man and kicks out at all around him. The past was infinitely better in all its aspects, at least until he gets his way (and a spaceship). At which point there's a major tonal shift as he heads out on his mission. Deidra is more likeable – also bored with the inaction and resignation of her ultra-constrained society she's our inquisitive eyes and ears. I'm glad she's there, but the logic in her being allowed to go to space with Malefant eludes me. But the real head-scratcher for me is Earth's reaction to its future destruction. Space colonies are abandoned and the end is considered inevitable, since only Earth can a properly viable habitat for mankind. But surely not! Wouldn't we (mankind) try to push Shiva (the Destroyer) off its course? Wouldn't we try much harder to set up space colonies that worked? Or leave for different star systems? Or work on trans-dimensional gateways? When they're actually discovered on Phobos there's not even a 'never thought of that' moment, and certainly no speculation that the gateways they do discover could be used to save Earth's dwindling population. So yes, once again, maddeningly, Baxter's instincts about what might happen differ wildly from mine, which means I'll probably be thinking about all the angles in this book in ten years time, just like I still am with *Flood*. But, frustrating though it is at times, I did like this book and will certainly be looking forward to the sequel.

Bone Silence
Alastair Reynolds

Bone Silence is the 'Third book of Revenger', so if, unlike me, you've read the other two, you'll have a passably good idea what's going on. For us newbies, we're swimming in an unfamiliar ocean, surrounded by friends we have no recollection of, reminiscing about a past we can't remember.

But we soon pick up the pace. The book is set in the far, far future when our sun is now the 'old sun' and people live in orbital habitats ('worlds') because all the old planets have gone (presumably swallowed by the sun as it moved into its expansion phase). We're in the 13th 'Occupation' (never quite got an explanation of that, except they seem to have happened on a cycle of 22,000 years) which gives rise to new civilisations with only hazy myths of what might have gone before. There are aliens too, and monsters that are part alien part human (unless I've read things wrong and the 'monkeys' the author keeps referring to are just that, and not some alien anti-human slur).

The plot revolves around the Ness sisters, heroines of the previous novels as they worked on a ship gathering valuable artefacts from orbiting 'baubles' and then fighting their way past an infamous pirate called Bosa Sennen, acquiring her ship along the way.

What follows is a mission quest and, frankly, a romp through the world (in the loosest sense) Reynolds has created. The sisters are skull readers – ancient alien skulls contain within them the power to communicate across vast distances – and the book opens with Adrana Ness seeking a skull to replace the one formerly used in her ship, presumably lost or damaged in the previous book. The skull comes with a price – passage for an alien 'clacker' to a place of safety in a 'spindleworld'. The alien is cranky and has enemies – mixed up 'muddleheads' intent on killing the clacker and the Ness sisters – so a chase across space ensues, all the way to the spindleworld Trevensar Reach, where revelations await.

This is a character-driven space romp, and the Ness sisters are delightfully rough around the edges. Fura, the ruthless one, is fighting with some alien 'glowy' inside her, intent on turning her into something else. Adrana, the conciliatory personable one, has to contend with a skull that doesn't work as intended, and a new crew that by rights shouldn't entirely trust her (since she crippled their ship on a pirate raid). For the Ness sisters, the journey is partially about redemption – for right or wrong, they are perceived as pirates and outlaws – but partially about proving themselves.

The first book in the series won a YA prize and the relative youth of the protagonists fits it nicely as such, though I think Reynolds wrote it with adults in mind - nothing to scare the horses though, give or take a severed limb or two. All in all it's pretty traditional space opera fare, albeit expertly delivered. Entertaining and fun. I just wish I'd read the other two books in the series first.

That's all for the first issue of *Wyldblood Magazine* - we hope you enjoyed it. The next issue will be out in March 2021 – available from www.wyldblood.com and Amazon in print, PDF, epub and MOBI formats.
Or why not take out a subscription? Check out www.wyldblood.com/magazine for details. £35 UK and £55 US and overseas for 6 issues.